WE NEVER KISSED

LIA FAIRCHILD

ISBN: 978-0-9864153-9-5

Chapter One

Alex

I trailed behind Lauren, her long legs balanced atop four-inch, deal-sealing black stilettos, as she glided behind the maître d'. I caught the scent of something flowery coming from her silky blond hair as it bounced on her bare back like drizzle on a windshield. She'd definitely made an effort. Maybe too much of an effort, considering how hard I'd tried to get a yes from her. The back of her dress was low cut, with enough skin showing for a craps table. But her beauty wasn't the only thing that had attracted me to Lauren in the first place. It was her intelligence, confidence, an air of genuineness that seemed to hint that she'd have no problem giving you a smile or the finger—depending on which applied more.

I let the host pull out her chair—only because he'd beaten me to it—and watched her gleam a fresh smile in thanks as she sat. Appreciative—I like that.

I secured the seat across from her, leaned back in my chair, and took in her beauty: smooth skin the color of damp sand, dark blue eyes blanketed in long thick lashes. The perfect woman for any man. So, why did I have to fight the urge to stare right through her as if she were a newly cleaned window? Why had she lost my attention in an instant? *Because your thoughts keep going back to* her, *idiot.* At least I'd thought it was her when I saw her in the airport earlier today. Even though it had been more than a year since I'd last laid eyes on Ava, I thought if she was coming home she'd at least give me a heads up. A text or something.

When the maître d' walked away, Lauren set down the menu he'd handed her. She folded her arms, leaned back in her chair, and stared right back, releasing a glare I could tell spelled trouble. "Well?" she said, brows raised.

I blinked, unprepared, and produced the best faux grin I could come up with. "What?"

"You didn't say anything about my appearance when you picked me up, you were practically mute in the car, and now it's like you're not even here. Are you not the same guy who gave me the full-court press just to get me to go out with you? *Best night of my life?* Or was that all bullshit?"

I could ignore the fact that Lauren instantly made this about her. Partly because she was damn right. I was acting like an ass. But that didn't erase the fact that I'd thought Lauren was everything I wanted, and now that I had her with me, something just felt...off. That wasn't her fault, though, so I leaned forward, noted the bumps on her exposed arms, and ran a hand down one of them. My eyes locked onto her gaze. "You look chilly. Let me get them to turn the air down."

Her expression softened at that, a sexy smirk materializing. "I'm fine. Feeling warmer already."

I grinned from the realization that it was just that easy to win her back. *But is that what I really want?* We both knew this wasn't anything long-term, and now was not the time for life affirmations, anyway. I'd made a commitment, and I damn well needed to make this night special for Lauren. She deserved at least that much.

With my menu closed in front of me, I watched Lauren pick hers back up and scan the page. She glanced up at me from time to time, appreciating the attention. "You on a diet?" she asked after closing her menu.

"No." I paused. "I already know what I want," I said, laying on the baritone for her.

It seemed to please her, and she let out a soft giggle. "So do I."

Eyes connected with hers, I was the first to break from the moment, turning to practicality. "Whatever you'd like," I said, then glanced around for the waiter.

We started with a bottle of pinot and a seared ahi appetizer, and I was finally able to relax some. Throughout the meal, we talked mostly about Lauren's job at a law firm. She shared her frustrations about being bored, uninspired, and feeling stuck under the glass ceiling of her traditionally male-dominated firm. "It's either a wedding or a new career, and I think we both know which one isn't going to happen anytime soon." She winked over her glass as she sipped at her wine.

Toward the end of the meal, she asked me about my company and the multi-billion-dollar deal that had been in the works for nearly six months. Of course that wasn't the reason she accepted my invitation to dinner, she insisted.

During dessert we shared Lauren's choice of strawberry cheesecake. Seductively, she fed me a bite from her fork and as I savored it, she surprised me with, "So, who is she?"

I swallowed, my gaze never leaving hers. "Excuse me?"

"Come on, Alex." She grinned and shook her head. My reaction must have been all she needed to confirm her suspicions. Another bite from the cheesecake, licking a dab of whipped cream from her mouth, was enough time for her to let me stew. "I'm not pissed, really. I can see that you're putting in the effort. But I know it's not your work that has you off your game, so the only thing that can cause a man to go so easily from hot to cold all night is the lingering thoughts of another woman."

"Seriously, Lauren, I..." *Damn, I hate lying.* Anytime I made an attempt, I ended up sounding like an idiot.

"Don't even try. Look, I'll be honest with you first. Maybe that will make it easier. I only said yes to tonight because my other plans fell through. A girls' night." She paused to gauge my reaction, then continued. "I was supposed to be in floor seats at the Lakers right now."

A mix of emotions played through my gut. I'd been in hot pursuit of Lauren for weeks, and this date felt like a big win. *Yeah, don't say that out loud.*

"Hey, I'm not saying I wouldn't have eventually said yes. I mean I am very attracted to you, it's just—"

"Are you always this brutally honest?" I cut in, even though I knew the answer.

"You know what?" She dug into the cake once again and offered me a bite to which I shook my head. "I don't have time for anything but."

Amused—and feeling slightly relieved—I chuckled. "I can see that."

She set the fork down, grabbed her wine glass, and leaned back in her chair. "So? Who is she?"

I thought for a moment, staring at the amazing woman in front of me, knowing my confession would kill the rest of the night. But if I were honest with myself, it had already flatlined, though I did think Lauren was someone I could be friends with long-term. And I didn't have too many of those. So, I took a leap. "Her name is Ava."

"I knew it," Lauren said, pointing a finger at me in an annoying little-sister manner. "What else? What happened between you two?"

Why did you have to open your mouth about Ava? The truth was complicated. I rarely let myself consciously think of Ava, and yet she always seemed to be on my mind. Like she had a lifetime lease in a little corner office in my brain. "Nothing," I said, and upon seeing the skeptical look on her face, I added, "Seriously... That's the problem."

"Unrequited love?"

"Not exactly." I blew out a breath. "Hell, I don't know. Maybe it is. But, with Ava it's more like..." I searched for the answer in the pool of red wine swirling in the glass I held. "Unexplored..."

She smiled. "Even better."

"I don't see how." All I knew was that for as long as I could remember, there was this pull that kept me tethered to Ava and all the memories we'd shared together. I had to constantly convince myself we were like family, and that was the reason. But every time I was around her, my heart raced like a freaking freight train, and I could say with one hundred percent certainty that never happened around anyone in my family, what little there was of it.

Lauren flagged the waiter with a head bump and a smile. "I'm going to need more information to respond to that one."

We ordered coffee, and I briefly pondered trying to salvage sex tonight, but we both knew it was off the table. Surprisingly, I didn't hesitate to share my story with Lauren. It was one that needed a voice and was long overdue. Maybe I could talk my way out of Ava before I actually ran into her in person. So, I settled into my chair and started, "She was my best friend's little sister..."

"Now we're talking," Lauren said, her expression delighted. "Only one of the most popular romance book tropes."

"Great, I'm a cliché." I shook my head but still managed to chuckle at myself. The truth was the truth.

"I'm sorry, continue." She made a flourish with her arm.

"I remember walking into their house after playing basketball with some friends, and there she was. Sammy and I had just started hanging out, but we hit it off immediately. There weren't any instant fireworks or anything between Ava and me. In fact, I distinctly remember her sneering at me from behind the kitchen counter."

"Okay, this love story is going downhill fast." Lauren rolled her eyes, like I was a huge disappointment.

I was lucky she hadn't walked out with my admission about Ava in the first place. "You do realize we were just kids at the time, right? I was probably fifteen then. Maybe sixteen."

She waved a hand at me. "Fine, fine, then get to the good stuff. The sparks, like when did you guys get together?"

My frustration level was growing by the minute. Did she want to know about me, or was she just looking for some juicy story she could share by the water cooler? "Like I said before, we were never together." I shook my head, thinking of all the time we'd spent together over the years, how natural and right it all felt but at the same time, I just...couldn't. I had never been good enough for Ava, anyway, even if I felt it was all right to pursue her. "We grew close over time, but I went off to college, we lived our own lives, and each time we saw each other this...thing between us became more intense. It was like we were in a relationship that neither of us wanted to acknowledge." We also had these sort of ticks of time where we were texting, flirting, dancing around the thing between us. Typically, it was right after she stopped seeing someone. One of us would eventually stop answering until we started up again like no time had passed.

Lauren was shaking her head at me, so I stopped.

When she didn't say anything, I said, "What?"

"Sex."

"What about it?"

She leaned forward and rested her elbows on the table. "Alex...from what I know about you, and granted it isn't much, substantially speaking, Ava is like the ultimate prize. You love the chase. And it sounds like this has been a long one, about fifteen years, so just do it already, and that will probably solve everything."

I huffed. *Please don't let her be right.* I mean it was entirely possible given my track record, but... "No. You're way off base."

"How do you figure?"

I picked up my half-drank coffee and sipped the lukewarm liquid. "Let's just say I had some...chances at that. I could have had her—" I cut myself off, finding it difficult to even speak of Ava like she was some sort of business deal I was trying to close. But I needed to get this out, and I somehow valued Lauren's opinion, especially given how forthcoming she'd been. So, I started again. "Ava came to visit Sammy and me at college. She'd just graduated high school, almost eighteen. We'd had a party at our place, and Sammy let her drink, thinking he'd keep an eye on her." I paused, not enjoying the thought of how innocent she was back then. "I was about to hook up with this sorority girl"—Lauren rolled her eyes, but I continued—"but when I got back to my room, Ava was there."

"In your room?" Her eyes were wide; she was fully invested in this story.

"Yeah. She was so drunk. And she was wearing one of my shirts." *Fuck, seeing her like that...* Said someone spilled beer on her. Anyway, I got rid of the girl, thinking I better keep an eye on Ava. Nothing happened, but Sammy came in later and damn near tore me a new one."

"Ooh, protective brother. He single?" Her eyes lit up.

"Married."

"Figures."

I didn't tell Lauren how we had lain on my bed, Ava's head resting on my chest, my arm draped around her and me feeling like I had a national treasure under my wing that I'd protect with my life. It was in that moment, I knew I was screwed. "Anyway... What the hell was I saying?" I ran a hand through my hair. "This seems pointless. I appreciate you listening, but—"

"Wait a minute." She held up her hands, palms facing me. "Give me some credit, here. I've got this all figured out."

"Right, I'm a player who likes the chase. Got it."

"Yes, true. But there's another layer to this mystery that you somehow missed." She licked her full lips, and I got a glimpse of how much of a world-class jackass I was going to feel like going home alone tonight. "You haven't made a real move in all these years because you fear Sammy's disapproval. And you're probably afraid he won't think you're good enough."

"Bullshit." But even as I said it, my chest tightened. Sammy wasn't just my best friend; he was like a brother to me. My home life had been a disaster, and his parents had always treated me like one of their own kids. Still did. *Damn, she's right.* It wasn't just Sammy, though, but their parents as well. I'd never want to do anything to disappoint Sue and Denny. I glanced away from Lauren and stared across the restaurant. What I needed was a way to end this night and put us both out of this misery. When I felt Lauren's hand on my arm, I turned back to her. "I'm sorry. You were just trying to help."

She laughed. "I'm not some wilting flower you have to be careful around. I can take it. Besides, I'm not the one suffering."

Suffering? Narrowing my gaze at her, I said, "I'm not suffering."

"Okay, Romeo. She doesn't even live here, and you can't get through a date without pining over her? Maybe your other women are distracted by that sexy dark mane of yours and that five o'clock shadow, which I would have enjoyed, thank you very much—"

I gave her a head tilt, and my best devilish grin. "There's still time..."

Adding her own head tilt, she snapped, "Nice try."

"Gave it a shot." I shrugged, then added, "Plus, she might not live here now, but she is in town."

"What!" Lauren shot a look around the restaurant, realizing she'd said that a little too loudly. "Why didn't you say so? No wonder you're acting like a lovesick school girl." She winked, but it didn't soften the blow.

"Thanks..."

"Okay, here's what's going to happen. The only way to salvage this waste of a night... Don't give me that look, we both know it would have been incredible." She seemed to shake off the thought. "Get out your phone. You're calling her."

Chapter Two

Ava

I sat on a barstool at the kitchen counter, drinking coffee and watching my parents make breakfast and flit around each other without saying a word—something that almost never happened. And since neither of them said more than a few words and a greeting when I got home yesterday, I expected a barrage of questions this morning.

"What's going on?" I said to them both.

Dad glanced at Mom, then stuck his head in the fridge. "Anyone want juice?"

I cocked my head at Mom and lifted my brows.

"What, honey? We're just making breakfast." Her chin-length brown hair swished as she busied herself.

"Uh-huh. And did you both take a vow of silence or something?"

"No. We're just giving you...space."

I wrinkled my brow as my dad turned and seemed to be holding back a grin.

"Space for what? You guys are acting weird—even for you." I laughed, but my suspicions along with the bad news on the tip of my tongue didn't allow me to feel any humor.

My dad opened his mouth like he was going to say something, and Mom shoved a piece of bacon into it. "We're just excited—and a little frazzled—about our big anniversary party. But since you're here early, you can help us with all the last-minute preparations."

Dad was nodding and chewing, then swallowed and said, "Unless, of course, you're too busy?"

I gave them both the side-eye and then sipped my coffee. I noticed my mom's stare homing in on my mug, and then her eyes popped wide. She shot a questioning look to my dad, who just skimmed his hand over the top of his partially gray crew cut.

What the hell is going on with them?

"Did you poison this?" I asked, setting down the mug.

Dad shook his head and gave my mom a pointed look. "Enough of this, Sue." Then he turned to me. "She was looking for the ring, sweetheart. We facetimed with Mark last week, and we've been dying ever since. We assumed that's why you came home, to give us the news?" His face froze with a goofy, expectant grin.

"Mark didn't say—" I let out a breath. "Oh, my God. Did he ask for your blessing for—"

"Yes!" Mom rushed around the counter and grabbed my hands with hers. "Oh, honey, we're so happy for you. I'm sorry we couldn't wait for you to tell us." She pulled me into a hug, and when my gaze connected with my dad's, I couldn't hold it in any longer. My eyes filled with tears and dad's face fell. He knew me better than anyone.

Dad came around and pulled my mom back. "Sue...honey."

"What?" she said, somewhat affronted. "Can't I—"

"*Sue,*" Dad said gently and then gestured to me.

I shook my head. "I'm so sorry..."

Realization finally hit, and my mom's confused expression turned to concern. "Ava, honey, what happened?"

I wished I had an easy answer for them. I was seconds from giving them the "It's not him, it's me" reason, but that didn't feel entirely true. Sure, I'd never really found my way after college, which I went to simply because my parents felt it was the thing to do. I'd wanted to be a dancer, and I'd performed in shows while I went to UNLV and some after, before I got my job at SLA

Publishing. But my uncertainty about my professional life didn't apply to my personal life. "I don't love him..." Then I quickly added, "Not the way I should." Mark was a decent guy, good-looking, kind. We'd felt so comfortable from day one, which was probably why we grew close so quickly. But from that first day, there was something missing. Something I knew existed because I'd felt it before. It was powerful and amazing and addicting, and it also hurt like hell because I could never truly have it. But that was what I wanted. I wanted it all.

"Are you sure that's it?" Dad said, his tone firm. "He didn't *do* anything, did he?"

"No, Daddy. Nothing like that." I held back the tears I felt fighting their way out. Tears that weren't for what I had lost but for what my parents had lost. "I'm sorry if you're disappointed."

Mom rubbed my arms. "We only want you to be happy. And I'm so proud of you for knowing what you want and what you don't want." She took my face in her hands and gave me one of her dazzling smiles. "We'll make the most of this visit. We can do whatever you want." Her face lit up. "Oh, do you want to go to the hospital with me and hold some babies?" Mom was a dedicated RN, and I was always so proud of her.

I laughed and covered my mom's hands with mine. "That sounds nice, actually. But I have more to tell you."

Mom took a step back. "Oh?"

A knot formed in my stomach at the looks on their faces. I hated how much they worried about me. I was twenty-eight, and they still saw me as their little girl. "I'm moving back home." I realized how that sounded when it came out. "I mean not *home* home, although I might need to stay here while Gunnar and I look for our own place."

"Gunnar?" Dad practically shouted. "The naked guy?"

"Dad!" I whined. I met Gunnar doing shows in Vegas, one of which just happened to be burlesque. Gunnar prides himself on his physique. "He wasn't totally naked."

Mom ignored the whole Gunnar issue and said, "Are you quitting your job?"

"I was going to, but they said I could work remotely while I figure out what I want to do."

"Is that why you don't want to marry Mark?" Mom sounded concerned.

"I thought he was gay," Dad said.

"Mark?"

"No, Gunnar." Hands on his hips, Dad blew out a breath.

"Dad, he's not gay. He's fluid...and pansexual."

He backed away to the kitchen, then. "You're throwing a lot of stuff at us, honey. Can I get the Cliff Notes."

"People don't use Cliff Notes anymore. You do know how to use Google, right?"

Mom folded her arms. "You know what he means."

I sighed. "You're right. I'm sorry. One, I'm moving back to Ladera Ranch because I want a fresh start. I had a great experience in Vegas, but it's no longer the place for me. And Mark isn't the man for me. Gunnar and I have a lot in common." Upon seeing both their expressions, I said, "What? I don't mean that. And for Gunnar, he just likes people and doesn't concern himself with anything but an earthy connection. He asked if he could come with me, and I was actually really excited to do this with him." *So, please don't ruin it.* "Anyway, if you guys don't want us here, we can—"

"Of course, we do, honey." Mom rubbed my shoulder, then shot a glare over to my dad. "Don't we, Denny?"

"Sure. Just tell him to keep his clothes on."

I gave my parents a tight smile. "It won't be for long. I promise. And thank you for understanding. I'll tell you more later, but I think I'm all talked out."

"We're sorry about Mark, sweetheart," Dad said.

I couldn't help but feel bad for him. He liked Mark, and I knew both my parents wanted their children to have long and happy marriages like they did. My parents had married right out of high school, and yet they waited ten years to have kids so they could spend time just loving each other. "I'll go back and get my stuff at some point after your party." I hugged my parents. "I'm going to take a shower."

Before I got in, I checked my phone, which I hadn't realized had died sometime last night. My heart skipped a beat when I saw a missed call from Alex. Could he have known I was back home? I hadn't even told Sammy. I checked my voicemails and texts. *Nothing.* Disappointment filled my gut. At least I'd see him Saturday night at my parents' anniversary party in San Diego. We had a lot to talk about, but some of it I wasn't sure when I'd be ready to tell him. Most of all, I hoped he didn't hate me for what I'd done.

Walking into The Cozy Crumb, the first thing I saw was Sammy and little Dax at a table in the corner with a full-on setup of coloring books, toys, and snacks. My four-year-old nephew did a double take when he saw me, even though I visited often, and we face-timed regularly. When he realized it was his Auntie Ava, he dashed from his chair, sprinted over to me, and took a flying leap into my arms.

"Auntie Ava!"

What magic little ones had to put things into

perspective and lift you up when you needed it. "Hey, little man! How are you?" I swung him around, then carried him back over to his dad.

Sammy stood when I set Dax down and gave me his usual side hug. Sammy was your typical overprotective brother but minus any affection. He showed his feelings with humor and sarcasm. "Hey, Sis."

"Looks like you've got your own little day care set up here."

"Pretty much."

Just then Cass came from behind the counter. She and Sammy owned the bakery and split work and child care duties. "Ava! My favorite sister..."

I laughed when she hugged me because Cass had four sisters of her own, but she always told me I was her favorite and never used the term sister-in-law. I was sure she loved them just as much if not more, but she was the type of person to make everyone feel special. "Great to see you, Cass."

When she pulled back, she gave a look similar to the one my dad had given me that morning. *I will kill them.*

"Listen," Cass said when the bell for the door dinged and someone walked in. "Everything your mom wanted is boxed up in the back and ready to go." She waved in that direction as she and the customer headed to the counter, with Dax following. Cass was also crafty and offered to make the party-favors for my parents' fortieth anniversary party.

"Great," I said, relieved I didn't have to talk about the elephant in the room. I couldn't believe my parents told Sammy that Mark was going to propose. *Unless Mark had told Sammy?* Either way, it put me in another uncomfortable situation. Then again, it wasn't like I could avoid telling people we broke up, considering he wouldn't be at the party on Saturday.

I set my purse and phone down on the table and was about to head to the back when the bell rang again. Instinctively, my gaze went to the door, and I locked eyes with the man coming through it. Just like every damn time, he took my breath away. Light blue eyes against a backdrop of honey-colored skin and jet-black hair, thick and wavy. I knew I'd see Alex at the party, but I wasn't prepared for this so soon.

Walking toward me, he never pulled his gaze away—not even when he stopped right in front of me. "Ava..."

That one word—in his deep silky tone—paralyzed me. We just stared at each other for what felt like way too long for the audience of people who knew us. Snapping out of it, I steeled myself and managed to offer an awkward hug. "Alex... I didn't expect to see you here."

One side of his mouth curled up, as if he were delighted that my voice shook. "I'm here all the time."

Though Sammy and Alex lived very different lives, nothing ever touched their bond. And the biggest thing they had in common was me. Those two were like a little mafia, Sammy being the head and Alex the muscle. If a guy had even looked at me sideways, well... Dating wasn't easy.

"Uncle Alex!" Dax screamed from across the room. Then he proceeded to give Alex the same greeting he gave me.

Traitor.

When Alex set him down, Dax asked, "Are you here to play wiff me, Uncle Alex?"

His eyes darted to mine for only a beat before he looked away, allowing Dax to take him by the hand to the table. "No, I just stopped by to see if I can do anything for the party."

"I want to go!" Dax whined.

"I'm sorry, buddy. It's a grownup party. You're going to stay in the hotel room with Aunt Sadie and her kids."

Sadie was probably the only sister of Cass's that Alex hadn't slept with, and that thought sat in my gut like a ton of bricks. Everyone knew Alex was a player, so why was it I couldn't function like a normal person around him? Why the hell would I want to be another cog in the machine that kept Alex's bed warm? The truth was there was a side to Alex most didn't see. A side that spoke to me and made me feel like I was the only one who truly knew him.

"Why don't you help Ava?" Sammy said. "There's a couple boxes in the back you can both carry to her car."

"Sure thing," Alex said before giving me a head nod and then taking off toward the back.

Wordlessly, I followed in his wake, admiring the slight stretch of his dark-gray business jacket across his broad shoulders. We each grabbed a box and made our way out to the street where I'd parked Dad's SUV.

As we loaded the boxes into the back, I filled the silence. "I got a missed call from you last night…"

We faced each other, and my pulse quickened at what I saw in his eyes. I couldn't exactly place it but it wasn't anything pleasant. I could always tell when something was wrong, though.

"Yeah… I, uh, just wanted to offer up my help, for the party." He rubbed a hand over his jaw.

"You knew I was already here?"

He nodded. "Sammy told me."

More staring. More silence. It hadn't always been like this between us. Sometimes we'd felt close…too close. Then one of us would back away. Sometimes the sexual tension was off the charts. But this… It was like a game of chess but neither of us knew the moves.

"How's Mark?"

My eyes widened for just a beat, and I swallowed. "He..." *Tell him.* If anything he should be happy. Sammy and Alex always seemed to celebrate my breakups. Meanwhile, Alex never had them—because he never kept a relationship going.

Seconds ticked by, and then Alex's phone rang. He yanked it out like he was a gunslinger at a showdown. Looking at the screen, he said, "I'm sorry, I have to take this." As he stepped onto the curb, he turned with a tight smile and said a quick, "I'm happy for you, Ava, really." Then he walked away.

Son of a bitch. He thought I was engaged.

Chapter Three

Alex

I sat at the hotel bar, pre-drinking before The Steadmans' anniversary party. Yes, I could have done it in the privacy of my hotel room, but that just seemed pathetic. Plus, I might as well take advantage of the fact that, like many of the family members, I was staying in the hotel, so I wouldn't have to drive all the way back drunk and tired. I'd actually checked in a day early to meet with some business contacts I had in San Diego, so it worked out all around.

I took a sip from my glass of Angel's Envy—I did enjoy a nice bourbon. Not that drinking alone was common practice for me. But I'd fucked up. Missed my chance with Ava once again. And the thought of spending the evening in her presence... Well, disabling a half dozen brain cells was all I could think of. I just had to be careful not to ruin the family's night. Because they were my family too. The only real family I had. Sue and Denny were there for me when my own parents weren't—couldn't be. The Steadmans had gotten me through some of the hardest times in my life.

I still couldn't believe Ava was getting married. When I chickened out and didn't leave her a voicemail, I'd called Sammy right after to see it was Ava I'd seen at the airport. And when he dropped that bomb on me, I'd had to make an excuse about an important call coming in because I couldn't fucking breathe. Felt like I got sucker-punched in the gut. As close as Sammy and I were, I'd never once let my feelings for Ava show. Because I knew I could never act on them.

I glanced over my shoulder to the ballroom, where the doors were propped open and a sign sat near the entrance that read: *Congratulations, Sue and Denny, on 40 Years!* What made it more amazing, is that they'd married right out of high school.

As if I'd willed them to appear, the happy couple rounded the corner and were heading right toward me. I slid off my bar seat to greet them. Sue was wearing a Champagne-colored skirt and matching jacket, and Denny was in an all-black suit like me.

I hugged them both, and Sue kissed me on the cheek.

"You look stunning, Sue."

She tapped my lapel. "And you're not only handsome but full of shit."

"No, honey, he's spot on this time." Denny squeezed his wife's hand, a loving expression on his face as he gazed at his wife.

Those two were the epitome of relationships. Maybe because they gave themselves a solid ten years together before they had kids. I couldn't imagine ever having what they had.

They both faced me then, their smiles radiating not just happiness but a love I could feel deep down. Part of me felt guilty for dwelling on losing Ava when it was their night, but I was also grateful to be a part of this amazing family.

"Listen," Sue began, taking my hand. "You can say no if you want, but the kids are each doing a toast, so we'd love if you said a little something too."

"Oh..." I placed my free hand over my heart, totally caught off guard.

"We know how you love to take over a mic," Denny said with a crooked grin.

"Hey, that was one time. And I was still learning to control my liquor." I gave a single head nod. "I'd be honored to. Thank you."

"We love you," Sue said, and Denny nodded.

"See you in there, Son."

I watched them walk away before returning to my seat, a lump making its presence known in my throat. I was damn lucky to have them. Maybe Ava getting married was for the best. If she and I ever got together, I'd screw it up for sure. I couldn't bear the thought of losing her or anyone in the Steadman family. An image of Ava in her wedding dress, dancing with Mark popped into my head, and I took another healthy sip to wash it away.

I ordered one more and took my time finishing it as I waited for the guests to fill the room; maybe I could disappear among the crowds. Still, all eyes would be on me when I gave my toast. But there was only one pair of eyes that could destroy me tonight, and as I glanced over my shoulder, the woman who owned them was gliding toward the ballroom.

Fuck me.

Ava was naturally beautiful and typically wore little makeup, but tonight she could have just stepped out of the pages of a magazine. The gown she wore was a dark and elegant shade of red, almost burgundy. It hugged her curves to perfection and had one sleeve draping her arm in sheer red material. The floor-length dress had a slit that I had to tear my gaze from before I broke out into a sweat. I actually eyed the path that led back to the elevators, but now was not the time to turn tail and run.

I stalked after her, planning to...I wasn't sure, but as she entered the room, I saw dozens of eyes turning her way —men and women. A sense of urgency shot through me; if I had the guts—and was the selfish bastard I wanted to be —I would drag her out of that place and take her back to my hotel room, where we'd stay until I properly worshiped her the way I'd only dreamed of.

I said her name, and she stopped short, hesitating a beat before she turned to face me.

Closing the distance between us, I said, "You're breathtaking, Ava." I'd never used that word in my life, but it felt appropriate and inappropriate all at once.

She grinned, but it only lasted a moment, and I knew something was coming. "Can we talk?"

"Dance with me," I said without thinking. I took her hand and led her to the dancefloor but before we stepped foot on it, fear shot through me as my mind flew back to another time I'd held Ava in my arms.

Chapter Four

Alex

Six Years Ago

I held up a glass of champagne as I addressed the ballroom, toasting to my best friend, Sammy, and his new wife, Cass. I talked about how we met on the basketball courts at sixteen and how Sammy could do a layup like nobody's business, even though he was only slightly taller than Kevin Hart. Everyone laughed and knew I was exaggerating. I tried not to get too emotional but shared how the guest room in casa Steadman was basically my bedroom whenever I needed it. And that was a lot. What I did not share was late-night trips to the kitchen, hoping I'd run into Ava—which I did sometimes. Or how many times over the years, I'd dated someone to forget about her. Sadly, it created this image in her mind of the kind of person I was, and I never corrected her. Hell, maybe I was that guy.

I raised my glass higher. "To the beautiful couple and the long, long, loooong"—everyone laughed—"journey you're starting today."

The night carried on with food and dancing, including the one designated for best man and maid of honor, which had me paired up with Cass's sister Elsie, whom I'd slept with the night before. We were both drunk, and I felt like an ass afterward. But as luck would have it, Ava caught the bouquet, and I caught the garter, which meant we were to dance together too.

I stiffly took Ava into my arms as the crowd around the dancefloor watched before joining in. An adorable grin played on her face, but it was when she brought her gaze to meet mine that everything and everyone fell away.

"We really only have to do this for a couple minutes," Ava said, flitting her eyes away. "Once the others join us we can stop."

I pulled her a little closer, showing her I disagreed. "You got somewhere to be?"

"No..."

We stared into each other's eyes without talking, but it wasn't awkward at all. It felt like we were holding a conversation with our eyes...and our bodies. But then a sudden need to hear her voice took hold, and I said the only thing I could think of. "How's the show going?" Before she could answer, I blurted, "You still seeing that tool, Eliot?"

She laughed because we both knew no one she dated would ever be good enough in her brother's eyes or mine. That was one of the great things about being friends with Sammy. I could always blame my jealousy on him. And it was an added bonus that Ava was terrible at picking guys. "What if I am?" she said with a defiance in her eyes.

I pressed my hand firmly into the small of her back. *Mine,* I wanted to say. "I don't like him for you."

Ava leaned in until her lips were near my ear. "You don't seem to like anyone for me, Alex."

I breathed into her hair, wanting so badly to tell her how I felt. I'd stopped myself so many times from telling Ava I wanted her, had wanted her for so long, because I knew what a disastrous mistake it would be. But this night felt different. She'd just graduated college. She was a grown woman who could take care of herself. *But you'll never be good enough for her.* And that was as good a reason as any.

Ava leaned back to catch my stare again. "Nothing to say, Alex? No smooth comeback?"

"You're perfectly capable of making your own decisions. I need to stay out of it."

She coughed out a small laugh. "Wow, how politically correct of you." Her expression didn't match her words, and I could see the hurt in her eyes. Sometimes it seemed, Ava wanted the same thing I did, and yet...she never said a word either. Her silence was another reason.

"Ava..." Her name came out harsher than I'd meant.

She took her eyes away and glanced around the dancefloor. "Actually, Eliot and I broke up. So, maybe I need to have a little something with one of these eligible bachelors tonight. Help me move past him?" She gave me a pointed look. "Sound like a good idea to you, Alex?"

"Damn, Ava, really?"

"So it's okay for you to be a... I won't say *manwhore*, but oops—did I say that out loud?"

I shook my head, not wanting to let her goad me. "You're better than that."

Her brows furrowed. "Says who?"

"Me. And I'm just trying to protect you."

Ava dropped her arms then, and we stood in the middle of everyone dancing, staring at each other in a standoff. She folded her arms and let out a sigh. "So, you don't want me, but you don't want anyone else to have me either?"

I almost gasped at her declaration. We didn't say things like that to each other. Not directly anyway. "You don't think I want—" I dropped my head and shook it.

"What, Alex? Just tell me for fuck's sake."

"You know I care about you, Ava."

"Do I?"

I wanted to say it, so desperately it burned a hole in the back of my throat, in the depths of my gut, and pierced through my already struggling heart. I was just about to step closer to her when someone appeared beside us, and I felt a hand on my arm.

"Finally, I was about to cut in."

I turned and found Elsie standing there.

Shit.

Elsie draped an arm around my shoulders. "Ava, you don't mind, do you?" Ava rolled her eyes, but it didn't deter Elsie, who added, "On second thought, why don't we get out of here for round two."

I watched Ava's eyes narrow, first on Elsie and then on me, hatred burning in their depths. "You guys have a good night," she said, staying focused on me so I knew exactly what that meant.

I should have chased after her; I wanted to, but I didn't. I also didn't dance with Elsie, at the wedding or between the sheets that night. All I cared about was that Ava didn't hate me. But the truth was...it was probably better if she did.

Chapter Five

Ava
Present Day

The first thing I noticed when Alex pulled me close was how he smelled. It always amazed me that the man could smell like home and desire all at once. I closed my eyes for a beat to let it sink in, to calm me for the conversation we were about to have. If only we could dance and simply be in the moment.

When I opened my eyes, he was so focused on me it was too overwhelming, so I leaned in and rested my cheek against his shoulder, letting myself get my bearings with him. Being so close and yet never feeling close enough, made my heart clench, and my throat felt like it was closing up.

We swayed in silence a bit too long because I was having second thoughts. Alex and I were better when we weren't talking. Sharing the same space with him had always been... It was as if he were oxygen, breathing life into me. I would have these flashes in my mind, these fantasies of what it could be like. Maybe the reality, if it ever happened, would be a sheer letdown, but my gut told me otherwise. When we would part ways each time, there was a crash—worse than any hangover I'd ever experienced—which I got through by diving into my life, staying busy, and yes, being with someone else. Mark was comfortable and the deepest I'd ever gotten into a relationship before breaking it off. But it was time to put all my cards on the table because I was tired of living half a life...of being without Alex.

"Well let me get a word in edgewise," I heard Alex say, snapping me out of it.

I looked up and let out a small laugh. "Sorry..."

He grinned and of course I melted, forgetting how to use words.

I drew in a deep breath, never taking my eyes off him, garnering strength from his solid frame pressed against my body. "I know what Sammy told you...about Mark."

Getting it out was harder than I thought, and with my hesitation came his words. "I'm sorry he didn't let you share the news, but like I said...I'm happy for you."

I gave him a head tilt. We'd never spoken any words to each other about our feelings. Hell, I could have dreamed up this whole thing in my head, a school-girl fantasy of a boy turning into a man before my eyes, but in reality he only thought of me as his friend's little sister. Frustration grew in my belly at the casual way he threw it out there. Did he owe me anything? No. My head might believe there was never anything between us, but my heart said otherwise. "Are you really?"

"Why wouldn't I be?" He gave me a tight smile. "I know me and Sammy were hard on you over the years, but you're an intelligent woman and Mark, well, he's... He's a decent guy."

I shook my head. "Wow, way to throw in the towel in the home stretch."

Alex's eyes darkened and his hand tightened around my waist. "What do you want me to say, Ava? At some point, I have to butt out and let you live your life. And if marrying this guy is what you want, then—"

"It's not!" My eyes widened at hearing my defensive tone. I drew in a breath to settle my nerves. "Mark didn't propose."

"What?" His face showed he was clearly shocked.

"He asked my parents for their blessing. I guess they told Sammy too. They were excited..." I felt my face flush with embarrassment. "He never got the chance to ask."

"Well, shit... I don't know what to say. I'm sorry?" His eyes darted around us as if he were seeing if anyone was listening. "Wait... What do you mean he didn't get the chance to ask?"

My heart pounded so loudly in my chest I wondered if he could feel it against his own. "I broke it off."

Alex sucked in a quick breath, pressing his chest harder into mine. "Oh... Well, I'm sorry, Ava." He glanced away.

"You keep saying that. Are you really?" It was several long beats before I blew out a frustrated breath, and he returned his gaze to me.

"No." He chuckled. "I'm not sorry. Is that what you want to hear?"

"Can we stop this, please? This is like six years ago all over again. I broke it off with Mark because I didn't love him the way I knew two people should love each other. There was something missing. Just like there was with every other guy I've been with. You know what I'm saying, Alex?"

"Yes." His breath grew heavy, and the emotion in his eyes was evident, but still he hesitated. "But..."

"But what? One of us needs to stop being so damn cryptic and spell this thing out."

One side of his mouth turned up. "Go right ahead."

"You ass," I said, half playing half serious.

"We both know it's not that simple. You, Sammy, your parents. You all mean...everything to me. You're all I've got. I can't fuck around with that."

My heart felt like it was going to tear in half, like he was going to move us from this ten-year dance to closing the door forever. At the same time, I cared enough about him that I didn't want anything bad to happen to him either. "So, what do we do? Keep living like this? Maybe instead of having a boyfriend, I could just be like you and jump from bed to bed with no feelings involved?" I regretted it as soon as the words came out. Just like six years ago, only slightly less childish. "I'm sorry," I rushed to say.

"Trust me, I know how hard this is. And maybe if—"

"I'm moving back home," I blurted.

His eyes widened with fear, and it was like a punch to the gut. *God, is he so afraid of the possibility of us?*

We stared at each other while I let him process that. I could tell the song was ending, and I wasn't sure how it would look if we continued dancing. The thought of that alone made me realize Alex wasn't the only one concerned about the implications of us being together.

"It's a special night for your parents. Maybe this isn't the time or the place..."

"You're right." My heart sank. It was a convenient excuse. "I shouldn't have expected—" I cut my own sentence off when I saw someone heading toward us just as the song was ending. Elsie walked up to us and said, "Hey, you two. Déjà vu." She laughed and slipped a card into Alex's pocket. "Thank you. Found my earring." And then she walked away with a sly grin.

Panic in his eyes, Alex turned to me.

I shook my head. "You've got to be fucking kidding me."

As I sat at a table, glaring a hole in Alex's back, I sipped a glass of Champagne, feeling anything but bubbly. I knew I shouldn't be pouting at my parents' party, but I was giving myself until this glass was finished to get over it. After all, it wasn't like I didn't know exactly who Alex was.

Just as I downed the last sip, my phone alerted me of a text. I quirked a grin when I saw it was Gunnar, one of the only people who made me smile lately. Gunnar was like a brother, sister, and BFF all rolled into one. We both loved to dance and perform. We believed in giving back and volunteered together once a week at the food pantry. And we both secretly hated *The Bachelor*. It never bothered me he commanded all the attention when we went out, his wardrobe much more stylish than my own, and his face resembling a runway model.

Gunnar: *So, are we going to be homeless or did Mummy and Daddy come through?*

Me: *We're in! But are you sure it won't be too awkward for you?*

Gunnar: *Honey, I've lived in an all-boys school, stayed with my nana and her lover, and roomed with a bunch of strippers. I think I can handle Mr. and Mrs. All American.*

I laughed because I was the one who played up my parents as perfect. And even though they'd been a bit hesitant for us to come and stay with them—albeit temporarily—I knew they'd welcome Gunnar with open arms. Plus, dance people were used to chaos and sharing bathrooms.

Me: *They're going to love you just like I do.*

Gunnar: *Bitch, don't make me cry when you're not here to hug me.*

"Who's Gunnar?" I heard over the loudspeaker and jumped. *What the hell?* I turned in my seat, left then right. Sammy was standing behind me with the mic in his hand. Apparently, reading my texts over my shoulder.

"You jackass," I whispered. It wasn't that I was hiding Gunnar from them, but I also rarely talked about the life it didn't seem like any of them approved of. It wasn't until I started at the publishing company that I began to share more with them.

He ignored me and said into the mic, "Will the owner

of a blue"—he made a pouty face—"Gremlin, please come and move your daughter. She's about to be towed."

Laughter rang through the crowd, and I shook my head. I reached up to grab the microphone, but he whipped it out of my reach and laughed, like the annoying big brother he'd always been. Then back into the mic, he said, "Seriously, Sue and Denny have requested everyone to get on the dancefloor. You know what time it is, people!"

Great. I was so not in the mood for the Tush Push, but I also didn't want to disappoint my parents. I waved a hand at my brother. "Yeah, yeah." But then I laughed. The Steadmans didn't let pouting linger. I knew it was time to give in.

As a flood of people moved to the dancefloor, I scanned around to see where Alex was and more importantly, where Elsie was. I still couldn't believe those two hooked up again. For all I knew it was a tradition or something. Like a long-term booty call.

My parents took their spot in the front, where I typically was as well, helping anyone who wanted to join in but struggled with the steps. Thanks to Sammy, Mom knew just where I was and looked over at me, giving me a head tilt. I blew her a kiss and stood but then pointed to the back. She shrugged and didn't seem to be unhappy about my choice. I was relieved they were both having such a good time.

From the back I could keep an eye on Alex, who was only a couple rows in front of me, without being ambushed. He was no Gunnar, who could easily go from a choreographed Vegas show to freestyle in a nightclub. But Alex still looked sexy as hell. I couldn't seem to stop myself from staring at his ass as he moved to the music, having removed his jacket. My brain was conjuring up what it would be like to experience those moves up close and personal.

As if he sensed me behind him, he glanced over his shoulder, and our gazes locked. We exchanged a soft grin, and it felt like he knew I wasn't mad at him anymore. It wasn't like Alex owed me anything. At the next turn, Alex stayed facing the back—and me—and made his way over to do the dance next to me.

"So, who is Gunnar?" he said beside me.

"Someone very special to me." I grinned, enjoying making him squirm.

"Is he why you broke it off with Mark?"

"Partly..." I shrugged. *If he was going to say dumb shit to me then I wouldn't correct him.* Plus, it was partly true.

Alex didn't like that answer based on his expression. I should have stopped but after that crap with Elsie, I was in the mood to be petty. So, I sidestepped closer to him, and said, "We're actually moving in together."

His hand gripped my elbow, and he said in my ear. "Like hell you are."

I stopped and glared at him until he released me. Then I said, "That big brother act is getting stale," before I walked away.

Alex was hot on my heels as I headed for the exit, and the song ended.

"Ava Steadman!" My brother's voice boomed over the mic.

I stopped and spun around, Alex reaching me and stopping as well.

"Some important announcements, please..." He went on to thank everyone for being there tonight and sharing my parents' special night. It seemed he was ready to wrap it up when he said, "And since my wife's family is heading back tomorrow morning, names will be drawn to watch Dax tomorrow while me and the missus get some special time." He tucked the mic under his arm, and mimed turning a bingo wheel, then pulling out a ball. "And the winners are..." *Don't say it. Don't you dare say it.* "Ava Steadman...and Alex Bannister! Don't forget to collect your prize. One small boy."

Chapter Six

Alex

$\mathcal{I}$ woke with a start, my heart beating double-time, the pitch-black room making me wonder what the hell time it was. The clock was turned the other way. I remember the annoying light keeping me up, so I'd knocked it away.

I sat up, wiping beads of sweat from my forehead. *Was it the dream again?* I couldn't be certain. All the signs were there, but I couldn't remember what I'd been dreaming about. I fell back against my pillow, taking it as a good sign. And yet, as I lay there, I began to replay the memory responsible for my nightmares. Sitting in the back seat, my mom driving, hearing her crying. She'd picked me up from kindergarten and said we had to go far away. The fear I'd felt when she told me that was dwarfed by the chaos that ensued only moments later, leaving me scarred both mentally and physically.

"Dammit!" I blew out a breath, angry with myself for thinking I could change what had happened, just by trying to change the memory. It was never going to happen. I hadn't spoken to my mom in a long time. So long, I wasn't sure I'd recognize her voice. In some ways she was a stranger to me. Last I'd heard she was dealing cards and trying to stay clean.

I reached over and turned on the lamp, then searched for my phone. I found it under the covers, which meant I fell asleep texting with Ava. It wouldn't be the first time. I didn't have a death wish, and despite the fact that she'd basically called me out, I still wanted to make sure she was all right. I also tried to give her an out for today, said I'd take care of Dax myself. Another thing that wouldn't be a first. She'd replied with a laughing emoji. It probably only pissed her off more, but I reminded her that I had actually spent more time watching Dax than she had.

The hotel we were in was more elegant than family-friendly, but after I grabbed a quick shower, we found a quaint café, and the three of us sat down for brunch, despite the fact that Dax had already eaten breakfast. Like me, the four-year-old was grumpy when he was hungry, so too much food wasn't a concern on this day. And with his parents off to spend some quality time together, there weren't many options for entertainment.

"What would you like to eat, sweetie?" Ava asked Dax.

He didn't answer. Dax had an assortment of Hot Wheels in front of his booster seat that kept him busier than I'd expected or preferred. Dax behaving meant Ava and I had to talk. I would have much preferred staring at her and enjoying her toned dancer arms and lightly tanned skin. The floral sundress she wore was both sweet and sexy, and it was killing me.

"It's fine. I'll order for him," I said.

Ava furrowed her brow. "Why you?"

I leaned back in my chair, lifting a brow in challenge. "Go right ahead."

That was clue enough I had no faith in her to accomplish the task successfully. But she picked up the menu and perused it, as if she knew exactly what she was looking for.

Holding back a grin, I said, "Need a hint?"

She tilted her head in Dax's direction. "Cheerios?"

Dax rolled a car up Ava's bicep.

"Eggs?" Her eyes darted from Dax to me.

"Psh!" I shook my head.

The server, whose nametag read Angela, stopped in

front of the table just as Ava said, "You're just trying to screw with my head!"

"I'll give you another minute, then." Angela backed away.

"I'm guessing she won't be back for a while. I'm starved too." I shook my head again, tsking, laying it on thick.

"Aw, does the grumpy baby want some Cheerios while they're cooking his food?" Then she picked up one of Dax's cars and pushed it in front of me. "Here, play with this to keep you busy."

Dax gave me a big grin. "Uncle Alex, play cars with me!"

Ava's eyes widened at how loud Dax said that, but I was used to it. For some reason, in the last few weeks, he'd been exploring his tone and often shouted his words instead of speaking them. Ava's gaze went over my shoulder, and then she winced. "Shh, honey, we're in a restaurant."

"It's a café," I corrected. "And he's just a kid."

Tilting her head, Ava said, "That man behind you gave us a dirty look."

"So."

"So, I don't want Dax to see his Uncle Alex manhandle a disgruntled diner. Plus, we should let him do whatever he wants?"

I shrugged. "First of all, that was a long time ago. Second, not whatever he wants... But you of all people should be more patient and understanding of this behavior."

"What's that supposed to mean?"

I leaned forward, taking my time to answer as I enjoyed the irritated look on her face. "Well...you're a creative, a dancer."

"*Was* a dancer—"

"You'll always be a dancer, Ava," I said pointedly, pushing away images of Ava on stage, elegant and beautiful at times, downright sexy other times. "And Dax is expressing himself."

She laughed. "And how do you know that?"

"I just do. Squash him now, and you might just be dashing the talent of the next Pavarotti."

She scoffed. "That's a stretch."

"Look, are we ever going to order? Dax likes toast with butter and jelly and a couple slices of bacon on top of it."

"Ew, really?"

"Yeah! Bacon sandwich!" Dax threw both hands in the air, and in the process, the car flew from his hand. I followed its trajectory and watched as it landed on the next table over, right on top of Mr. Dirty Look's eggs. He pushed his chair out, stood, and turned to us.

"Well, this'll be fun," I said to Ava before standing to face the guy.

"Alex, no," I heard Ava say behind me.

Not that Sammy and I went around looking for bar brawls, but we'd been in our fair share of scuffles. That, however, was not what triggered Ava's concern. She was remembering about five years back, when I was in Vegas for a bachelor party. Sammy hadn't wanted to leave Cass, because she was pregnant with Dax, but I still made a point to check in on Ava. I'd misjudged the situation. I could see that now. But when I had seen hands on her, and she didn't look happy about it, I saw red. Without hesitation, I'd flattened the guy. Ava had been embarrassed, sure, pissed too, but more than that the fear on her face was like a knife to my chest. I never wanted to see that look on her face again.

So, I would keep my cool.

"Alex..." Ava rasped out again.

"It's fine," I threw over my shoulder. Then I faced the guy, made eye contact, and said, "Sorry, man. Let me ask the server to bring you another one."

The guy in front of me was about my height but a little smaller in build, short blond hair and pale skin. "Damn right you will. Looks like you need to control your kid *and* your woman."

What the hell?

The woman he was with picked up the car and gently set it onto our table before sitting back down without saying a word. I gave her a nod and heard Ava tell her, "Thank you."

"Look, man, he's just a kid, and it was an accident," I said, not hearing much sincerity in my voice. "Are your damn eggs so important to you that you need to get in my face?"

"It's not just the car. He's been loud as shit since you got here. Keep it down, and we won't have a problem."

I had a choice to make in that moment. Sure I could apologize, again, promise to keep Dax quiet, which I knew wouldn't happen. Or we could find another table, or even just leave the café altogether. But this guy was pissing me off. I'd done the right thing, and he wasn't having it.

So, instead I leaned in so only he could hear me. "Look, I tried to make it right, but I think you just want to be a dick. Now if I wipe the floor with your face, my woman is going to be pissed. But I'm willing to risk it, if you don't get out of my face right fucking now." I only pulled back enough so he could see in my eyes I meant it.

He maintained eye contact for about ten more seconds before he pulled back. "Whatever..." He turned away, saying, "I don't have time to wait for more food. Let's go, Dee."

"We'll get your bill," Ava said before I could.

The couple left without further incident, and Ava and I exchanged sly grins. Dax was none the wiser, which was good because I didn't want him tattling to Mommy and Daddy. When the server returned. I took care of the couple's check, then the three of us ordered the Dax special plus two hot chocolates: one for Dax and one for Ava—her favorite. I knew all Ava's favorites. Despite spending years in different states, I felt like I knew almost every damn thing about her.

Which was why I found it strange that I'd heard very little about this Gunnar guy. I didn't have time to pump Sammy for info, and the only reference I could pull from my memory banks was something Ava's dad said a few years back after a visit to Vegas. He talked about someone with an unusual name—could have been Gunnar. I wasn't about to ask Ava. Not yet anyway. I was too busy watching her sip hot chocolate and grin like a school girl.

After the café, we walked to the beach, since the hotel was just a block away. We both wanted to give Sammy and Cass as much time alone as possible, given that they rarely took time away from the bakery. Truth be told, I never wanted the day to end for selfish reasons.

The three of us strolled along the boardwalk, Dax between us, holding each of our hands. It was a vision I'd allow myself to picture only on rare occasions. Ava's dark hair blew across her face with the slight breeze, and I wanted so badly to brush it away, run my thumb over her lip, then draw her mouth to mine.

She grinned when she caught me watching. "What?"

I shook my head. "Nothing. I was just enjoying hanging out with you...without the drama, that is." I flashed her a crooked smile, but it didn't soften the blow.

"Drama? Wait a minute..." She scoffed. "Which one of us is responsible for drama?"

I lifted one shoulder. "Not me?"

"Funny because I was about to say the same thing."

"What's drama?" Dax said, trying to skip faster than we were walking.

Ava and I exchanged surprised glances, as if we'd both forgotten little ears were listening.

"Why don't we get you something to drink, buddy?"

"I'm not firsty. I want to play in the sand."

We stopped and moved aside from the flow of pedestrians. Ava eyed my jeans, tennis shoes, and polo shirt. "It's fine with me but..."

"I don't mind. Whatever he wants."

"Yay!" Dax took off, dragging Ava behind him.

I slipped off my shoes and socks and followed them.

Dax wasted no time plopping down in the sand close enough to the water he could get his hands on the damp stuff. I loved that Ava didn't hesitate, even though she wore that cute sundress that looked like it could be new.

At the party she was elegant and beautiful, but she also didn't mind getting her hands dirty. There was nothing I didn't love about her, even if she was an annoying pain in my ass sometimes.

The three of us sat in the sand, Dax simply attempting to build the world's tallest hill. Sandcastle wasn't on his radar yet. Dax talked about the part-time preschool he started, his favorite shows, pretty much anything he could think of, and it was fine with me. I got to look at Ava without the pressure to have any real conversations—not that I thought I could avoid it forever.

"Aunt Ava, look!" Dax held a tiny crab in his hand and then set it on Ava's leg.

She yelped and jumped sideways, crashing in to me. I caught her, and when she looked into my eyes, my heart stopped. If only I could just hold her, stare into the depths of those chocolate brown eyes, and then...

"Sorry," Ava said but made no attempt to move, her dark gaze telling me she wanted me to kiss her. Right here. Right now.

It felt momentous and risky and something I couldn't stop myself from doing because it was all I wanted in that moment. I felt her chest heave into mine as we both leaned in closer to each other.

Just before I closed the distance completely, I saw two tiny sand-covered hands land on Ava's cheeks. I pulled back and watched as Dax planted a long pressing kiss on Ava's mouth. "Mwah! Bride kiss!" Dax called out. It was the term he used after seeing a couple kiss on TV at a wedding.

Damn, I just got bested by a four-year-old. I couldn't help but bust out laughing. Ava's shocked expression was almost worth missing out. But I wouldn't make that mistake again. The next time I had a chance to kiss Ava, I would damn well take it.

Chapter Seven

Ava

Despite sitting in a comfy recliner—more luxurious than any furniture in my apartment in Vegas—I squirmed as the plane hit a bit of turbulence. I stared across at Alex, who didn't appear to have an ounce of worry in his gaze, in this ridiculous private plane. Alex said it was called a Gulfstream and that I would be much more comfortable than in a commercial aircraft. I found it to be the opposite.

I didn't know what the hell I was thinking, but somehow Alex had talked me into flying with him to Vegas. I had planned to fly back after my parents' party, finish packing what little things I had, and then drive back with Gunnar, who didn't have a vehicle. That was still the plan for the way back.

"Are you sure this is okay?" I said, nervously clasping my hands in my lap.

"Well it's too late now," he said with a chuckle.

Alex apparently had this big deal in the works, and one of the companies involved owned this jet and sent for him. He worked for an investment banking firm, and according to Sammy is one of their top dogs. Sammy could have been there right with him but chose a different life. Sometimes I wondered if Alex didn't want any of the traditional things Sammy chose for himself. Our conversations never got that deep. No, I didn't just wonder it; I feared it.

"Like I said, they told me to pick when and where— somewhere midway between us—so I said Vegas. I guess you're lucky the timing worked out, huh?"

"Yeah, lucky," I said with a bite to my tone because what I really felt was awkward. Without Dax as a distraction, we were forced to either address the elephant in the room or dance around it, like always.

"I know you're not afraid to fly, so..."

"In this plane? I mean, didn't you see any of the movies about famous people dying in planes like this?" He made a face and I continued, "Buddy Holly? Jim Croce? Ritchie Valens?"

"Since most of those were decades ago, I'm guessing this plane is a lot safer…"

I stuck my tongue out at him.

"I could come over there and hold your hand if you want?"

He might have been teasing me, but the thought sent a wave of heat through me. If he were paying attention, he'd see it on my cheeks. "Let's just change the subject, okay?"

"Fine with me…" He stared at me a moment, as if he were debating asking me something.

"What?" If ever there was a time to do this, now was probably best. I braced myself for his next words.

"Talk to me about this Gunter fellow, and why I haven't met him."

Now that I hadn't expected, and I let out a laugh. "What are you, my daddy?"

"Do you want me to be?"

His deep tone sent a thrill through me, and my pulse quickened. Alex had a way of drawing me in and then scaring the shit out of me. I wasn't sure how I was ever going to navigate this thing with him. It was like standing at the edge of a canyon, wondering how the hell you could make the leap across. With my mouth hanging open, I searched for what to say. When he lifted a brow in challenge, I steeled myself. "First of all," I said matter-of-factly, "it's Gunnar, and secondly you did meet him."

"Guess he made quite an impression on me."

"Well, most people who meet Gunnar never forget him..."

One side of his mouth quirked up in a sexy smile that made my heart pound. "Maybe I was distracted..."

"Anyway... We've actually known each other for a long time. Well, we danced together for a long time, but we only grew close in the last couple of years."

"And you guys never..." Rubbing his jaw, he watched me intently.

"No! I mean, we might have had a drunken make-out session once, but we realized we were so much better friends. We have a lot in common, but we both really bonded over doing charity work. Instead of regular coffee dates, we volunteer together." A nervous energy in my stomach told me I was in dangerous territory talking about my volunteer work. I'd been hesitant to bring up Alex's mom, and yet as long as I don't, it feels like lying.

"Can I ask you something?"

I nodded.

"Since I've known you, you've always wanted to help people. You always loved volunteering at the hospital with your mom, and now you're doing this charity work with Gunnar. So, why are you working at a publishing company?"

"Because I have a degree in English…and Mark helped me get the job."

He looked thoughtful then, and I hoped he wasn't judging me. The days of Alex trying to tell me what to do were over. But then he surprised me with, "You're an amazing woman, Ava, and I think your heart is telling you which direction to go in. You left Mark. Maybe it's time to leave that job too."

"God, I hate it when you're right." My eyes popped wide. "Shit, did I say that out loud?"

"I'm afraid so."

That sexy grin was shining bright, and all I could think about was him leaning over and pressing his mouth to mine. My breath grew heavy as we gazed across the small space.

"Alex," I said at the same time he said, "Listen…"

We laughed but before either of us could continue, the captain announced our descent.

"That was fast," I said, even though I knew LA to Harry Reid was a quick trip. My heart sank as realization set in. We would go our separate ways, and I wasn't sure when I'd see Alex. I'd be home in a few days, but then what? If he wasn't ready to talk about a relationship, then clearly he wasn't ready to have one.

Once we landed and were given the all clear to remove our seatbelts and get our bags, disappointment poured over me. What did I think was going to happen? That Alex would profess his love to me, take me into his arms, make love to me right there on the plane like in some romance movie? Any or all of the above would have been nice...

Silently, I reached for my small carryon and slung it over my shoulder, avoiding Alex's gaze. He was in front of me, so I couldn't move until he did. When his fingers touched just under my chin and nudged it up, I startled, eyes wide as they connected with his.

"What's wrong, Ava?" He said it softly, and his sincere concern cut like a dagger to my heart.

I shook my head, afraid to say the wrong thing but more scared of not saying anything.

"You're upset...at me?" And then he grinned.

"Is this funny to you?"

Alex released my chin and ran his hand down my hair, stepping closer so our bodies brushed against each other. "No," he whispered, his lips near mine. "I was just thinking about the irony."

"Of what?" I said, breathless.

"The last time you were mad at me at an airport."

Chapter Eight

Ava

Four Years Ago

It was a little after two in the morning, when I raced down the hall of the hospital and fell into Alex's arms. Without heels on, my five-foot-five frame practically disappeared within his six-foot-two stature, with his broad shoulders and solid chest. All the panic and worry that had built-up on the plane flight over, as well as the subsequent cab ride, was still present, but I no longer felt alone in my worry. Just the feel of Alex's body against mine comforted me in a way I knew no one else could.

When we pulled away, I saw the wetness from my tears on his dress shirt. "Any news?" I asked.

"They're both still in recovery. Your brother is with

Cass—she's still unconscious—and the baby is in the NICU with your mom, so he's well taken care of."

Cass had been just three weeks shy of her due date when she was in a car accident. The seatbelt and airbag that were designed to save your life proved detrimental to both her and the baby. Cass was unconscious, so the baby was delivered by C-section.

"Where is everyone else?"

"Elsie and Sadie went to get food, and your dad went home to change and let out the dog. I told your parents to get some rest, but you know them. I said I'd wait here for you, though." He guided me toward some chairs in a seating area, but I stopped short before we sat.

"No, I can't sit. That's all I've been doing." I shook my head. "If I can't see anyone, I need to keep moving."

"We can wander around the halls, get some stale coffee?" He glanced around and then hurried to add, "Actually, this place is depressing. Let's go outside. It's a little chilly, but they have a nice garden area."

We headed down the hall and toward the exit. "Wait," I said, stopping and turning to him. "What about you? Do you want to go home? You've been here all night, right?"

"I'm fine. I don't need anything." He gave me a tight smile and a brave face.

"You have work tomorrow, though." Alex was only a couple years in at his investment banking firm, where he'd interned while getting his MBA. Rising to the top was his singular focus, and from what Sammy had told me, he was not only their rookie of the year but quickly becoming one of their greatest assets.

"Ava, this is my family, too, and I'm not leaving until I know they are both all right."

My eyes glossed over then, not only from the promise that left me speechless but at thinking about the prospect of losing either one of them.

"Oh, God, Ava. I didn't mean... They're both going to be fine. I know they will." His arm slid around my shoulders as we left the building and walked onto the dimly lit pathway that wound around the hospital.

Alex kept me distracted by asking me questions about the show I was in, how long I would keep dancing, and about my new boyfriend, Mark. Surprisingly, he didn't give me his usual third degree about a guy I was dating, but instead of being relieved, I felt disappointment wash over me.

We checked our phones constantly as we walked, and eventually, found a bench to sit on. I didn't hesitate to lean against his strong shoulder and accept the comfort he offered. At some point, I must have dozed off because both of our phones pinging startled me. Glancing at the time, I saw I'd been out for almost two hours while Alex held me.

We both read the group message from Sammy,

alerting us Cass was not only awake but out of the woods. Little Dax's vitals were strong, and there was a picture attached. A sob of release shot from me. "Thank you, God," I whispered as Alex pulled me into a hug. For some reason, I was crying harder than when I got there.

"Hey, it's okay," Alex whispered against my hair, one hand behind my head, the other pressed into my lower back.

So many emotions combined with the fact that being this close to Alex was both overwhelming and comforting. I allowed myself a few more minutes before I reined myself in. When we pulled apart enough that I could look him in the eye, I said, "I'm sorry. I'm such an idiot. This is wonderful news."

"Stop it. You've had a long night, Ava. You're entitled."

I gave him a heartfelt, "Thank you" and then before I could stop myself, "I don't know what I would have done without you—"

"Don't... Please, don't make me out to be something I'm not." Guilt laced his tone.

"How can you say that? I don't know why you do that to yourself, Alex. You're an amazing man..."

He pinned me with his dark gaze, drawing me in. We stayed that way, our breathing heavy, for several long beats. His thumb brushed the wetness from my cheek before both hands took hold of my face. "God, Ava, why..."

His words barely registered. I couldn't make sense of them with how intensely he stared at me. My heart felt like it was going to explode. "What...?"

He still had ahold of my face, and he pulled me closer, leaned down until his lips were a breath away. "I've tried so hard, Ava. Dammit, I've tried..."

When his lips brushed against mine, I gasped and pulled back, my gaze narrowing on him. "Are you fucking serious right now?" *All the times I dreamed of kissing this man, and he does this now*...when I'd just entered a serious relationship, and I was still reeling from Cass's accident. I rose from the bench, steeling myself so I wouldn't start crying again. "I have to go..."

Alex didn't try to stop me, didn't say a word. Thankfully, mine and Cass's family members filled the waiting room, and even when we visited Cass, Sammy, at least, was in the room. I stayed until the sun rose, and with a heavy heart at not being able to hold my new nephew yet, I arranged for my flight back.

I was in line at the security check when I heard my name being called. I turned to find Alex speed-walking toward me. "Is everyone okay?" I said in a rush before he even reached me.

"Fine. Everyone is fine." He paused a moment to catch

his breath, as if he'd run all the way from the parking lot. Then he surveyed our surroundings. I was in line between a teenage girl and a couple speaking what sounded like Dutch. I wasn't about to get out of line so whatever he came to say would have an audience.

"I fucked up?" he said, one hand in his pocket, the other roughing through his messy head of thick hair. "I know you're pissed at me, and you have every right to—"

"Don't tell me about my feelings, Alex. You can't even manage your own."

The woman must have known some English because I caught a smirk before she turned away.

"I know." He shook his head, his face wrecked in desperation. "It can't be shitty between us, Ava. Please, just say you forgive me so things can go back to the way they were."

Yeah, because things were so freaking great before. What choice did I have? Alex was part of our family. He was Sammy's best friend. We all had history you don't just forget about and move on. I pulled my lips under my teeth and stared at him. *Dammit*, I couldn't lose this man no matter what was or wasn't between us. So, I said the only thing I could. "Okay."

Chapter Nine

Alex
Present Day

Her lips were so close to mine it wouldn't take much to close the distance, to finally capture her mouth and show her everything I had been wanting. Everything I prayed she wanted too. I had fought it for so long I felt paralyzed as I wrestled with my decision. Just staring into her dark eyes tore me up inside. It was Ava, for God's sake. The perfect woman. The perfect woman for me. But at the same time, all I wanted to do was protect her...and maybe that meant protecting her from me.

The thought grated against my desire for her. *Why can't I have her, dammit?*

I knew the reason, but I was quickly losing the battle. And when Ava reached up on her toes, snapping me back to her, it was all the motivation I needed. I bent to meet her, pressing my lips against hers, my palm brushing over her cheek as I slipped my other arm around her waist, pulling her closer. Her eager mouth moved in perfect synchronicity with mine, as if we'd done this thousands of times—and yet it felt like I'd never kissed anyone before. Her arms snaked around my neck, one hand caressing the back of my neck.

It only took seconds before her lips parted for me, and I deepened the kiss, hearing a quiet moan escape her. All other thoughts left me as I reveled in the moment, and we both instinctively pulled at each other to get closer, yearning for more. It was everything I'd dreamed of and more.

But an untimely cough behind me had us pulling apart.

"I, uh, I'm sorry to interrupt..."

I turned to find the captain standing there. He glanced at his watch. "I can give you a few more minutes..."

"Thank you." I waited for him to go back to the cockpit before I faced Ava again. "That was unfortunate," I said somewhat awkwardly. My heart was still racing, and my eyes whipped down to Ava's mouth for just a beat before making eye contact again. We'd just had something momentous interrupted, and I was already feeling a sense of loss. I wanted to touch her, hold her. Would I ever get to again? She was still standing right there, but it felt like she was miles away.

Ava only nodded at my comment, so I had no idea what she was thinking. Did she regret it? Or maybe she was waiting for me to take the lead on the whole "us" situation. Instead of doing that, I took her hand in mine and gazed at her. *Say something, you coward.*

Giving me a slim smile, she said, "You don't have to say anything." She squeezed my hand. "We don't have to jump into anything either."

Was she giving me an out or was that coming from her gut?

"I know. I just..." I was flailing, and she knew it by the look on her face. I wasn't prepared for this. Never thought this dream would come true.

Seeming to read my mind, she said, "Look, Alex, it took us fifteen years to have a first kiss..."

"So, what are you saying? We should wait another fifteen years to get to heavy petting?"

She laughed, and instinctively I dove in and pressed my mouth to the corner of hers. I was already taking liberties I shouldn't, especially if I couldn't back them up with the right words. I was so fucked. "That doesn't count as number two." I smirked. "Seriously, what are you saying? Where do we go from here?"

"Let's not overthink it. We both know what this is."

We do?

"But, Alex, I have to go and end one life so I can start a new one." She pulled the bag back onto her shoulder that had fallen off when I kissed her. "And I'm going to have Gunnar with me when I get back."

Hearing his name, despite what she'd said about him, put me on high-alert. "Yeah, speaking of that guy, are you sure—"

"Seriously, he's like a brother to me."

I quirked a brow at her, pointing out the irony. "Really?"

"You know what I mean. Let's just say Gunnar really loves fruit, like every kind of fruit. Even peaches. But his favorite is banana, see?" She showed me an adorable grin as she moved past me.

I grabbed her arm to stop her. "You said we don't have to jump into anything. What if I want to jump...?" *What the hell are you saying?* Ava and I together, like really together, was one of my biggest fears. I knew I'd screw it up, and where would that leave me? I'd practically be an orphan. I ran a hand through my hair, knowing I was already screwing this thing up.

Thankfully, her head tilt told me she wasn't taking me seriously. "I just got out of a long-term relationship and you... Have you even ever had one?"

"Define long term." I winked at her.

"Oh, yeah, you're ready for this, Alex..." She shook her head. "Let me get my life in order. We'll...keep in touch, see how things go, okay?"

Wow... Ava was calling the shots and so casually. I felt like I was riding the bench. I knew I'd think back on this when I was in bed tonight and wonder what the hell happened.

I saw Ava off, giving her a hug before she got into an Uber. Just for good measure I texted her moments after she drove away: *Say hi to Gunter!*

She replied with a laughing emoji, then wrote: *You'll love him... And you better call him by his correct name.*

One kiss... That was all it had taken to throw me into a tailspin. Ava was right to pump the brakes. So, why did I feel like every emotion I'd ever felt for her...just rose to the surface and demanded to be acknowledged and accounted for? Everything I had pushed back and told myself wasn't real suddenly consumed me.

I had to switch gears, though. I had a meeting with my clients, and despite riding the bench with Ava, I was the star player, running the show on this deal since day one. I couldn't drop the ball now. Still, on my way to the hotel, I couldn't resist texting Ava one more time. *That kiss, though...*

Chapter Ten

Alex

Sitting at my desk, I enjoyed a rare second cup of coffee since my 10:30 a.m. conference call was canceled. My mornings typically flew by with no breaks: a 5:00 a.m. wakeup, checking emails from home, then I'd hit the gym, shower, and then off to the office where I'd start with two back-to-back meetings, the second one being with my team. Some might find my schedule too hectic, but I reveled in it. I'd earned my spot at this firm. I went from analyst to associate in less than two years and associate to VP in less than three. It wasn't unheard of but it was rare.

Bringing my own deals to the table was the best part of my job, and the one I was currently working on, would go a long way to solidify my value. Which was why I had been in Vegas. Except for not getting to see Ava again—despite being in the same city at the same time—the trip had gone exceptionally well, and I definitely planned to take a breather once everyone signed on the dotted line.

Would Ava be ready to spend some time together then? Was I?

I sat back in my chair, a smile curling my lips. Typically, I took the occasional moment to gaze out my window, but on this day, I pulled up an image of Ava on my phone. Had I dreamt that kiss? It didn't seem possible that a little more than a week ago, I'd held her in my arms, something I'd only dreamed of doing.

I still held a crapload of reservations about any future that looked like us being together. A war waged inside me —fighting to have Ava as mine and convincing myself it would never work. That I'd fuck it all up, and the Steadmans would abandon me.

While I held very few memories of my biological mother, Sue was the one who received the Mother's Day gifts and the flowers for no reason and could call me away from work just to help her carry boxes in from the garage. And Denny...he was more like a father to me than the man I had lived with, who had often been away and was barely present when he wasn't.

I swiped from the image of Ava and pulled up my

message thread with her, my finger hovering over the screen. I'd never hesitated with a woman I wanted, but with Ava it was so much more complicated, and it had me questioning every decision. This was why staying busy was a good thing. Despite my reservations, I tapped out a message:

Me: *Where are you?*

Ava: *Who is this?*

Me: *Very funny.*

Ava: *Gunnar and I are out looking at apartments. Remember I told you that...*

Me: *Oh, yeah I forgot. How is it going? Any good prospects?*

Ava: *Good, yes. Affordable, no.*

Me: *But you're still working right?*

Ava: *I am, but editorial assistant doesn't exactly bring in the big bucks. I haven't really been dedicating a lot of time to furthering my career. And even though Gunnar is a trust fund baby, he's tired of living off his parents and then hearing about it afterward.*

I had to admire that, but until I spent some time with this guy, I wasn't about to start doling out compliments.

Me: *Maybe you need to look outside Ladera Ranch.*

Ava: *Trust me, we are.*

Me: *You know, you could let me help...*

Ava: *What are you going to do, be my sugar daddy?*

Of course, I knew she was joking, but the thought sent my mind spinning and my pulse kicking up. It wasn't how things were supposed to be these days but if that was what Ava wanted, I'd give it to her. I'd give her anything...

Me: *Well...*

Her reply was a series of emojis ranging from surprise to laughter and a few I didn't know the meaning of and wasn't about to ask.

Me: *I meant I have some connections both in real estate and publishing.*

Ava: *Thank you, but seriously, I have to do this on my own. Mark helped me to get my job, and I don't want help anymore. I need to do this on my own.*

Me: *And you will. I have faith in you. You are a strong and determined woman, and you can do anything you set your mind to.*

Three dots jumped for a minute, and I wondered if I'd said the wrong thing, even though I couldn't see how.

Ava: *Apartment manager is coming back. Gotta run... Talk soon?*

I didn't get a chance to reply before my phone rang, and I immediately answered it.

"Alex Bannister."

"Alex Bannister! Answering his phone, and on the first ring? Did you get canned, sweetheart?"

I let out an uneasy breath. "Not even close. You just got lucky."

"Oh, you know how I love to get lucky…"

"How are you, Jessica?" I replied, ignoring her innuendo. Jessica tended to lay it on thick whether she meant it or not. And it was a dicey line to balance on with her since her father owns one of the companies in a deal I'm brokering. She's sort of unofficially involved, but the way she constantly flirts with me makes me forget that we are supposed to be doing business together.

"Listen, honey. I'm just having brunch with my dad, and he says the lawyers are taking longer than they should, but that's not necessarily a bad thing. I don't want you to worry."

"I wasn't. But I don't think that's the only reason you called."

"Of course not. I was just making sure we're still on for Friday night."

This was something I had been dreading. She'd been asking me for a dinner date to talk about another deal she wanted to present to dear daddy, and I finally gave in, but this really could complicate things with Ava. I had to tread lightly with Jessica and not upset the current deal, but I also wasn't about to be her boy toy just so she wouldn't tell her daddy to put the kibosh on our deal because of her wounded ego. If I were being honest with myself, before kissing Ava, I wouldn't have been opposed to sleeping with Jessica, but now...

"Looking forward to it," I said.

When I ended the call, I swiped back to the picture of Ava on my phone. Maybe I was reading too much into Jessica's motives. Maybe it was all about business, and that was just her way. One thing I was sure about—I couldn't tell Ava about this.

Chapter Eleven

Ava

I stared at the screen on my laptop, waiting for Alex to come back. He'd said he wanted to get comfortable, lose the suit he'd had on for more than twelve hours. My heart raced at the slim chance that he'd come back half-dressed, which I wouldn't have minded in the least. I heard him come back into the room—his bedroom—and then he crawled onto his bed, wearing gray sweatpants—*good lord*—and a black UCLA T-shirt.

"Miss me?" he said, his arm draping across his chest after he adjusted the level of his screen.

The way his bicep pressed the limits of his shirt had me wondering if someone turned the AC off. *Damn, this man is hot.* Facetiming wasn't something we had ever done much of, but given our circumstances, we both seemed to crave seeing each other's face instead of just texting.

"I figured you were primping…" I laughed.

He gave me a sexy half grin, but his expression might have had a hint of embarrassment. "I don't primp."

"Uh-huh. Your hair just naturally looks that amazing."

He ran a hand through his thick mane, messing it up yet somehow making him look twice as sexy. We stared at each other for a few beats before he said in that deep heady tone, "Well, I missed you."

He knew exactly what he was doing, and it was working. I pushed myself higher up on my pillow, nerves bundling inside me. I wasn't used to navigating this type of conversation with Alex, even though I'd had plenty of fantasies about him.

When I didn't say anything, still left speechless, he said, "Lower your camera…"

My heart pounded double time. "What?"

He laughed. "Your shirt… I want to see what it says."

"Oh." I let out a breath, then made the adjustment so he could see the words, which read: *Dance Your Ass Off.*

"Do I make you nervous, Ava?"

Yes. "No."

"You're breathing pretty heavy over there. What can I do to help you relax?"

"Alex, I'm not nervous..." I blew out a breath. "Okay, I am. You're not?"

His eyes darted away for a few moments, then, "You'd think... But seeing you, that kiss... Knowing we're alone right now. I'm feeling something entirely different."

Shit. "If you think something's going to happen right now..." I coughed out a laugh. "I'm in my parents' home."

"So, afraid you won't be able to keep quiet?"

My mouth fell open, then I looked away, shaking my head. After a moment, I turned back to the screen, leaned over so he got a nice view of my cleavage, and whispered, "You know what I think... You're all talk, Alex." Just to mess with his head, I ran a hand down my neck, then grazed the side of my breast. "I think you love the chase, and if I turned the tables on you, started taking my clothes off right now... you'd run for the hills."

His dark eyes had pinned me, taking in every word, and his lips parted yet he wasn't responding.

"Now who's breathing hard, Alex? Nothing to say? I mean doesn't a little secret cybersex with your best friend's little sister make you—"

"Whoa!" He shook his head and huffed out air. "Fuck, Ava, you had me right up until you mentioned your brother. Talk about sabotage. What are you doing to me?"

At first I laughed, hard, but then when I saw the

genuine look of concern in his gaze, I sobered quickly. "This is really a big deal to you?"

"Isn't it to you?"

I sat crossed legged and clasped my hands in my lap. "I couldn't care less what Sammy thinks."

"And what about your parents?"

I narrowed my gaze on him, wondering how he could doubt their love. "You should know after all these years, they think of you as a son."

Rubbing his chin, he said, "Exactly. And if we start something up and it doesn't work out, you still have them." The despair in his expression killed me.

"So what? We go back to Alex and Ava one point oh?"

"Shit, I don't want that either."

"What *do* you want, Alex?"

He adjusted himself so he was sitting like I was and said, "I want *you*, Ava. Always have. Always will."

Holy Hell. For a moment, my heart stopped yet my pulse beat like a drum in my ears. I knew I needed to respond, but it was all too much, especially so soon after Mark. Alex's gaze flicked away at my silence. "Alex..." When his eyes came back to me, I said softly, "I feel the same way..."

We stared at each other for several long beats, a longing in my chest aching to be near him, to touch him, feel his lips on mine again, to have him right here in my bed with me. "Maybe... we don't have to tell anyone. We figure out a way to be together, see how things go between us first."

A wide smile grew on his face. "I like that idea. Wanna come over?" He laughed. "Too soon?"

"I think so. But, what if I came over on Friday night? We have game night on Saturday so we'll see each other then too." As soon as I'd said it, I felt regret. Was I ready to be alone with him in his apartment? I knew exactly what would happen if I was.

Alex paused before his answer, his mouth tightening all of a sudden. "Friday will be...tough. Work stuff." A sense of relief washed over me until he added, "Maybe Sunday but we can confirm at game night..."

"Oh, okay." Even though I was hesitant, something about his response had me a little insecure. But then, he turned things right around.

"Great. But for now..." He winked, one corner of his mouth bumping upward.

"Alex, no..." I was tempted for sure.

"Okay, how about taking your top off."

I laughed with him that time. "Come on..."

As the two of us reined in our laughter, I must have missed my bedroom door opening, because Gunnar landed with a soft thump on the bed next to me.

"What are we doing?" He turned to my screen. "Oh, hey, good-lookin'," he said to Alex.

Alex and I both looked guilty, even though we'd literally done nothing of suspect.

"Hey, Gunnar," Alex said awkwardly.

"I'm guessing by the clothing and uptight faces I didn't miss the party." He grinned and lifted his brows. "You know, three beautiful people like us could do some serious damage together."

My mouth flew open, and I smacked him on the arm. "Gunnar!"

"Please tell me he's joking," Alex said.

"Sure, yeah, ha-ha." Gunnar scooted off the bed and walked to the door. "You guys are no fun."

When the door closed behind him, I said, "Maybe that's my cue to go."

"Wait, you mean I don't get to watch you sleep?"

I tilted my head at him. "It's not pretty, Alex."

"Oh, I know that." He laughed. "But I wouldn't mind. Since I can't touch you, I had other things in mind."

"Oh, my God!" I made a face, even though the prospect of Alex making do while he watched me was not unpleasant at all. "Have you no self-control?"

"Honestly, I don't know how I've done it all these years. You opened a door, Ava. The beast is out, and he's hungry."

Oh, God. I couldn't wait to experience all he was referring to, but I still played along. "Down, boy."

"I'm afraid it's too late for that. Goodnight, Ava."

"Goodnight, Alex."

Chapter Twelve

Ava

Gunnar reached across the table and pulled a massive pile of poker chips toward him with a satisfied grin splayed on his face. As he re-stacked his chips, he said, "Have y'all had enough, or do you want to rebuy?"

"Wow, make yourself right at home, Gunnar," I said with a giggle.

My mom pushed her chair back and stood. "If I had known you were bringing a card shark into this house, I would've said no." But then she ran a hand over the top of Gunnar's short brown hair like he was one of her own children and smiled at him.

It was strange how Gunnar fit right into our family,

doing things with us we'd done all my life. But instead of my brother at the table, it was Gunnar. He was just a naturally lovable person, and though he was unique in his own right, he was also a chameleon who could thrive in any situation. I was grateful he made this life change with me. It felt good to be home and made it less depressing that I'd ended a long-term relationship with a man who'd only treated me with kindness.

"Yeah, I think I've taken enough of a beating," Dad said, getting up from the table. "Anyone else want ice cream? I was going to watch some TV before I go to bed."

Gunnar and I exchanged silly grins. He and Dad had actually spent some time together in front of the TV, and though Gunnar wasn't a fan of football, the two found common ground in golf.

"I think I'm going to take the money and run," Gunnar said with not an ounce of guilt for taking my parents' money. I could only guess he loved the competition and the feeling that he'd actually earned that money.

"Yeah, I think I'm gonna do a little work and then go to bed," I said, then flitted my eyes to Gunnar, who shot me a look like he didn't believe me. I really was going to do work, but I also planned to check in with Alex and maybe pick up where we left off two nights ago. Not that I planned to get naked or anything, but I would like to try to figure this thing out with us. Alex's hesitation worried me, even if I understood.

We all went our separate ways, and I closed myself behind my bedroom door. I spent about an hour going through emails and reading some abstracts I needed to get to before I quit for the night. When I was done, I sat at my desk, contemplating going over to my bed before seeing if Alex was online. *That might be too tempting.* For me or Alex, I wasn't sure, but I had a feeling it would be both. My heart raced at the prospect.

I decided to try Alex, and if things naturally went in a certain direction, I'd make up my mind in the moment if I should take it over to the bed.

I considered texting first, but I was too excited to see his face, so I clicked over to our last video call and tapped it to redial. At three rings, disappointment settled in. I doubted he was asleep, but it was possible he was still working at the office, something he often did. Alex's schedule was nothing like a nine to five, and that was something else I had to consider. I wasn't sure how I felt about late nights at the office, taking clients out at night, flying out for business trips. Because all that equaled one question: would he even have time for a relationship? Assuming a relationship was what he wanted.

After a few more rings, the call seemed to connect, and as often happened, I heard the audio before the video kicked in. Only it wasn't Alex's voice; it was a woman speaking. Then I realized the video had turned on, but the screen was blocked. Or, rather, something was blocking it. *Is that...* I was staring at the back of someone's black dress, with the hint of black hair coming into the screen just past her shoulders.

My heart jumped at the thought of a woman being with Alex a moment before I reminded myself that there were plenty of women in Alex's office. He was probably working late. I also remembered he'd said something about having work when I asked if he wanted to get together on this night.

"Oh, hell, Alex! There's a damn gnat in my wine," the woman said.

Strangely, Alex's response sounded too far away for me to hear, which didn't make sense. Then the woman spoke again. "It's okay, I know where the glasses are." She turned then, and her large breasts spilling out of her dress filled the screen.

What the— That was not Alex's office. I could clearly see it was his apartment. Whether or not I had a right to be jealous didn't matter to the knot in my stomach and the fire burning in my gut. I watched as the woman set her glass down, then reached above the computer to the cupboard to retrieve a new one.

Alex must have walked into the living room because

this time I could hear him. "Sorry about that," he said. "Probably flew in when we were on the balcony."

What the hell were they doing sipping wine on the fucking balcony! My chest tightened, and it was hard to breathe, like a baby elephant was sitting on it. When my eyes glazed over, I pushed all my hurt feelings aside and berated myself for being childish. Just because I'd had a secret crush on Alex basically my entire life didn't mean he owed me anything. Still, the way he'd spoken to me lately... That kiss. I thought he wanted me. Only me.

And I was not about to watch Alex fuck some random woman on his kitchen counter. So, I closed the application and shut down my computer, convincing myself I hadn't changed my whole entire life for the possibility of being with this man.

Just then a couple of knocks sounded on my door before Gunnar opened it.

I turned my face away, throwing on a quick smile. "Uh, I could have been naked."

"And?" He came in and sat on the edge of the bed.

I joined him, switching gears to deal with this, something I knew could be an issue. I touched his hand as it rested on the bed. "We're going to have to set some boundaries if we're going to live together. You know that right?"

His mouth quirked up on one side. "I know. I'm sorry. I swear I forgot."

"You know what I'm going to say then."

He nodded, then recited the words I'd said to him recently. "Just because I'm comfortable with something doesn't mean others are."

"Very good." I gave him a smile.

And as the King of Switching Gears, Gunnar flopped back against my pillow. "But you're my bestie, so I get more than everyone else, right?"

I couldn't help but laugh, appreciating him taking my mind off what happened only a minute ago. "Absolutely... Just make sure you wait for me to say come in before you come in, 'K?"

"Got it." He patted the spot next to him. "Now come and tell Uncle Gunnar what's bothering you."

I let out an exasperated breath. "Shit!" Shaking my head, I crawled up next to him. "I hate that about you."

"No, you don't. Now spill, baby girl."

I gave him the blow-by-blow of my failed video call with Alex and waited.

Gunnar nodded for a few seconds before he responded. One thing he excelled at was breaking down a problem, unemotionally. "First...you don't know that anything happened or will happen, right?"

I shrugged.

"Second, you guys aren't even together yet."

I cocked my head, my expression saying, *Really?*

"Okay, you're right. But point one trumps that. So, really all you're dealing with here is that he lied." I started to speak, my mouth hanging open, when he said, "Unless... it *was* work."

"Sipping wine on his balcony, her in a damn cocktail dress?" I practically whined.

"Okay, that one the jury is still out. So, what are you going to do? Confront him? What if he doesn't even realize you called?"

Just then my cell rang. Gunnar and I exchanged wide eyes.

"See who it is," he said with urgency.

I swiped my phone up and looked at the screen. It was Alex.

Chapter Thirteen

Alex

I stood in the corner of Sammy and Cass's living room, nursing a beer and watching a dozen or so people race to stuff their faces before the games started. Sammy's game night had been happening for as long as I could remember. Even back in college, the guy could just as easily go to a frat party and meet women as he could spend the night in, playing board games or poker. The boy was competitive as fuck, too. And when he said we started at seven, that meant asses in seats by 6:59 p.m.

In attendance this time were Sammy's cousin, Terese, and her boyfriend, Keygan, some friends from school, two women from the bakery, and, of course, Ava and her attached-at-the-hip side-kick, Gunnar.

Dude looked like he belonged in a magazine ad for cologne. If I wasn't straight as an arrow, I'd find him attractive. *Okay, he's damn good-looking, and it bugs the shit out of me.* I just found it hard to believe he didn't still want Ava. Sure, she'd said nothing was going on between them, but that didn't mean he didn't still think about them. But who was I to talk? Plus, I had enough things to worry about where Ava was concerned: like how I was going to get her alone to explain about Jessica.

Sammy gave the ten-minute warning, and for some reason, that caused Ava's eyes to shoot in my direction.

I had been looking forward to this game night because it would have allowed me to spend time with her but, after what happened...the whole thing felt awkward.

I wasn't sure exactly what went down, but all I knew was that after I'd practically shoved Jessica out my door at ten thirty, I went to do some work and saw that there was a video call from Ava. After further inspection, I was shocked to find it had connected for almost two minutes. Who knew what the hell Ava saw during that time, but I had immediately called her. As I'd suspected she didn't pick up. I didn't send her a text because I wanted to speak with her face-to-face tonight.

I didn't know what I was expecting, but so far she was

acting as if nothing had happened. I supposed there could've been two minutes of empty air time, and there was no reason for her to be pissed at me, but that would be wishful thinking.

At the five-minute warning, Terese walked over to me, and we hugged.

"Mr. Big Shot, haven't seen you in a while." She sipped red wine and grinned, closed-mouth with full red lips. She'd always flirted with me over the years, but I thought she did with everyone. I'd made sure to keep a healthy distance just in case, since she was Sammy and Ava's cousin.

"Work's been crazy, but I'm not complaining."

I was about to ask how she'd been, when she touched my arm, and her face turned serious. "So, how's your mom doing?"

Her words hit like a gut punch, especially since they came out of left field. Most everyone there knew my history, knew about my mom, so I didn't get why she was asking me.

Just then, Ava rushed toward us. "Two minutes, people! Let's go." Then she looped her arm through Terese's, saying, "You're sitting next to me, cuz."

As everyone took their seats, I tried not to watch Ava's every move. Her dark hair, full and bouncy, covered part of her gorgeous face. The urge to reach over and brush it away made my hand twitch. She wore loose jeans that hung low on her hips and a tight black T-shirt with the perfect neckline to tease just enough. She had one of those magical smiles that made people feel cared for, and I wanted a big piece of that.

Despite the unresolved issue between us, I sat at the same table as she did, right next to Gunnar, whose grin was more of a smirk.

"Ready to get your ass kicked?" he said, and I caught Ava shooting him a glare.

At our table, Cass doled out cards for Cards Against Humanity while I had second thoughts about joining poker in the kitchen. What happened next didn't help my attitude.

Gunnar held up his glass to me. "Well fuck me six ways from Sunday...there's a gnat in my drink."

Shit. So, she had seen something on that damn video call and then went running to Gunnar? My jaw clenched as I ignored the man sitting next to me and focused on Ava. Her eyes caught mine for only a moment before she shrugged and picked up her cards.

Maybe I was reading into everything, but it felt like, throughout the game, the two of them took every opportunity to give me a dig or send me a message based on the cards they put out. But I made sure to remain unaffected; after all, I'd done nothing wrong, and I would explain that eventually. When that game ended, Gunnar stood and said, "I need some air. I think I'll hit the balcony." He turned to me, holding his glass. "Care to join me?"

"Naw, I'm good, bro," I said and gave him a healthy pat on the back, even though we both knew it was another reference aimed at me, since Jessica and I had been on the balcony. Then I laughed and added, "But there's no balcony in this house."

"Right..."

Ava came around the table then, but before she could say anything, I beat her to it. "You two have fun. I think I'll join the poker game so team play can be even." We'd had an odd number at the table, but the next game would be two groups battling it out in Pictionary.

My ego received a timely boost when I caught the disappointment on Ava's face before I walked away.

The poker game should have been more fun, especially since I came out ahead and Sammy was down— the perfect opportunity for me to rub it in his face. But thoughts of Ava had me off my shit-talking game.

At the end of the night Ava, Gunnar, and I stayed to help Sammy and Cass clean up. Working side-by-side, all I could do was fight the urge to take her into my arms and finish that kiss from the plane. Why was there always some issue between us? When she brushed by me, carrying glasses to the kitchen, I almost said something, but I couldn't bring myself to start that conversation with people listening.

Gunnar came out of the kitchen, carrying a bag of trash busting at the seams. "Here you go, big man. Cass says you know where this goes." He smirked, and it was all I could to tell that guy off. I was done with his bullshit. Then he winked at me, and I stepped right up in his face, ready to blow, when Ava appeared at his side, also holding a bag and giving me a pointed look.

Damn. I'd totally misread the situation. I took the bag from him, let out a breath, and stepped back, an apology in my expression.

"I'm on your side," he whispered before nudging Ava against her back.

We both headed out the front door and to the side of the house, wordlessly. And when I turned and opened the bin, we both threw our trash in and then spoke at the same time. I said, "I can explain," while Ava said, "You don't have to explain."

Reaching out, I hooked my finger into the belt loop of her low-rise jeans and pulled her snuggly against my body. "Please, let me say this, Ava." I stared into those big dark eyes, that stubborn expression I've seen so many times on her face, but now it made me want to crush my mouth to hers. I needed to make this right first, though.

"Jessica is nothing to me but a business associate. Actually, she is barely tolerable." Her face changed slightly, but it still said, *I'm not buying it.* "Her father is the one I've always worked with, but she is trying to prove something to him, and apparently that involves me." I bent my head until my lips were next to her ear. "I'm sorry I didn't say anything sooner." Then, I pressed a soft kiss on her cheek. I felt her grin, but when I pulled back, she quickly reined it in.

"So, you're saying nothing happened between you two? Even though you took her back to your place?" She laughed. "And, yes, I do realize I have no right to ask you that, but I'm doing it anyway."

Unwilling to release my grip on her, I used my freehand to brush my thumb over her parted mouth. "I'm glad you are. I don't want us to have secrets between each other, and I know this isn't the first time I've screwed up, and it probably won't be the last...but I promise you I want this to work."

Softly, she pressed her lips together over my thumb, her eyes still locked on mine. *Fuck, what I wanted to do with that mouth.* And when she bared down with her teeth—"Ow!"—I realized I still hadn't answered the question I said I would answer.

"The whole time, we talked business—"

"With wine...at your apartment," she cut in.

"Yes, at my apartment. There was some paperwork we needed to sign, and I didn't want to deal with security at the office, so we went to my place. And, yes, she was making herself way too at home. I should've done a better job at setting boundaries..." With both hands, I grabbed her by the waist and yanked her hard against me. "But my kitchen cupboard was the only thing she got her hands into, and I definitely wasn't in anything of hers."

That made Ava laugh, and I leaned forward and captured a quick kiss of her lips. But when I pulled away, she stood on her tiptoes to go back in for more, and I was happy to oblige, running one hand around to her lower back and then over her ass. *Damn...* I already knew I would never be able to get enough of Ava just by kissing her. I never wanted to stop, and I probably wouldn't have. But when she pulled back slightly, and her dark eyes found mine, a flash of light to my right caught my attention. "Shit, the porch light is flickering."

"That must be Gunnar. We better go." She started to move toward the walkway, but I grabbed her wrist and yanked her back.

"Wait. We need to talk about this. Another minute, please."

"I'm not mad. I promise."

She gleamed that beautiful smile, and I ached for more of it.

"I'm not talking about that. Look, Ava, I know how you see me, or at least how you used to see me." I ran a hand over my jaw. "And I get it, but I don't want to be that man anymore. I know this whole thing is strange, and you probably don't trust it, but to me it feels right."

She stared up at me, and when she didn't say anything, I added, "Uh, this is the part where you're supposed to agree with me."

My heart hung in the balance as she tried to back away, but I still had hold of her wrist so I laced our fingers together and gave her a half grin.

"Okay, I agree. I want to make this work too." She glanced down at the ground, and I wasn't sure if it was adorable or concerning.

My solution was to bend down and kiss her once again.

Quickly, she pulled back, saying, "But..."

"I had a feeling that was coming."

"Not that I want to be another one of your deals, but how exactly are we going to do this, especially if you don't want anyone to know yet?" She lifted her brows.

"Well...I do have my own apartment?" I lifted my brows right back at her.

"Not a chance," she said, shaking her head.

I had to admit, I felt a little like a scolded schoolboy. "Why? It's perfect." Just the thought of having Ava all to myself in my home, my bed... Heat raced through my veins.

"You know why." She glanced over to Sammy's house. "Part of not screwing this up is not just being discreet. It's not jumping into anything...and that includes your bed, Alex."

"Fine. Then what do you propose?"

She pulled her lips under her teeth, clearly having no plan herself. "First, I think we need to take it slow. We'll just have to figure out a way to spend time together, maybe none of the local places our friends and family hang out?"

"And second?"

"Well, you've proven to be a resourceful man, a hard worker... raced up the ladder at your firm..."

"And..." I wasn't sure what she was getting at.

"And...if I mean as much to you as your career does, then you'll figure out a way to make this work too." A sexy half grin tugged at her mouth.

Taking her by the wrist, I pulled her around the side of the house and pinned her back against the rough stucco-wall. "Is that a challenge?" I said against her mouth.

Her slight head tilt gave me the answer.

"You always were a pain in my ass, Ava," I said, grabbing said ass and scraping my knuckles on the stucco in the process. "But trust me on this, baby...when I really get ahold of your ass..."

She laughed right in my mouth. "Promises, promises."

I brought my mouth against hers, plundered her with my tongue in a long deep kiss before dragging my lips across her cheek to behind her ear where I sucked her skin in through my teeth. "I'll keep that promise, Ava." Then I slid away from her body, leaving her panting against the wall as I strode back to the house.

Chapter Fourteen

Ava

*L*ike two horny teenagers, Alex and I had been making out in the front seat of his car for the last ten minutes. Sure, one of us would try to get a word in here and there, but it always came back to our mouths needing to be connected, and his hands wandering dangerously close to the point of no return. We hadn't even started our first date yet, and I was letting him open me up like a cheap bottle of wine. *Going slow was your idea, hoe.* The reminder floated to the back of my mind, and in about ten seconds I was either going to climb onto his lap and literally screw that idea completely away, or I would have to jump out of the car and walk all the way home from Huntington Beach…a city I had no clue why we were in.

Thankfully, Alex saved me from either choice. Pulling away from me, he ran a hand through his thick dark hair. "Fuck, Ava…" Then he laughed. "I knew we should have gone right up."

I cocked my head. "Up? Just exactly where are we going?"

"You'll see." He opened his door, then turned back to me. "Wait, don't get out."

As Alex exited his black Mercedes, grabbed something from the trunk, and then came around to my side, I couldn't help but chuckle. "You're not serious with the chivalry thing, are you?" I said when he opened the door.

"I am actually." He reached his hand out to me. "But hey, if you don't like it, I'll shut the door, and you can do it yourself." His tone was stern. "I mean, I thought you'd like the best of both worlds, and I don't want to be a hypocrite when for all these years I told you every guy you dated wasn't good enough."

I eyed him from the passenger seat. "Interesting… And what would that look like exactly?" *I could get behind a little perch on a pedestal.* Shooting my arm out, I bent my wrist down like a princess waiting for a hand kiss.

"You know," he said, taking my hand and pulling me

out. "My respect and admiration, my acknowledgement of you as my equal, while at the same time, treating you like a queen."

"Hmm." Suspicious, I moved past him, and he closed the door. Then he grabbed my hand, and we jay-walked across the dark street, which was lit only by two of the four street lights that were supposed to be on.

I couldn't remember a time where we'd held hands, and it took me by surprise. The feel of it was so... I couldn't describe it, but it was almost like foreplay, and I grinned like an idiot. It was such a simple thing—holding hands—but it made me feel like...I belonged to him. Something I'd always secretly longed for.

We walked down the sidewalk until we came to a four-story building. He stopped us in front of the entrance and turned to me. His dark eyes squinted down at me. "Of course, there's one thing I left off..."

"You mean that whole chivalry thing?"

"Yes." One side of his mouth lifted, as if he were visualizing whatever he was about to say. "That doesn't include the bedroom, Ava," he said in a deep tone. "I'll worship your body, for sure, and I might let you take a little control...but if I want to take charge of you, whether that means I have to spank that sassy ass of yours to do it, then I damn well will."

My whole body flushed with heat, and my heart thrummed. This side of Alex terrified me...and I couldn't wait for it. "I, um..." My chest heaved, and there was a part of me that was irritated by that, and I fought the feeling because I didn't want him getting the best of me. That little girl mentality I'd grown up with around him would be tough to overcome. I drew in a breath and said, "Your offer sounds enticing. I'll let you know. Now, open the damn door and let me see what this surprise is."

We went up a few flights of stairs by the light of his phone, and to my surprise, Alex had a key and opened a door. I expected pitch black, but there was a faint glow coming from inside that let me make out a few features in the room.

"Oh, nice, so our first date is in what...an abandoned dentist office?"

Alex took me by the hand and guided me farther into the space. "Actually, it used to be a quaint little pub. Our firm facilitated a deal for this building—"

"And not only could you get fired for bringing me here, but you thought it would be fun to make out with trash and rats?"

Pressing up against my back, he slipped his arms around my waist. "Will you give it a chance? Look..."

My gaze scanned the room and landed on an area near

a glass window, and I gasped, sliding out of his grasp. Beautifully lit by electric candles and string lights, a small space was set up with a couch and a coffee table that was set for a meal, wine glasses and all. My heart clenched at the sight, and I turned back to him. "I can't believe you did all this." I shook my head as he moved toward me. But then he veered off to the side to something else that had lights on it, but I wasn't sure what the large object was that I was seeing. "Wait? Is that..."

Alex stood next to an old jukebox and nodded.

"It doesn't work, though, right?" I asked, hopeful.

Shrugging, he pressed a button, and music began to play but something sounded off, and I narrowed my gaze at Alex. Then he held up his phone and pointed to a portable speaker. "No, it doesn't."

I burst out laughing as he came over to me, then I snaked my arms around his neck. "It's perfect. All of it. Thank you." We kissed, slow and sensual, to the beat of some soft R&B tune. His hands delivered just the right pressure as he moved them over my back and hips and ass. I moaned into his mouth, and he lifted my thigh slightly so it draped over his. I wanted him so badly my head grew dizzy just from kissing him. But when his mouth moved to my neck, I saw a male form standing in the doorway, and I gasped.

"Alex, someone is here?" I whisper-yelled.

Alex moved swiftly, spinning around to face the doorway while at the same time, pushing me behind him, shielding me with his body.

I gripped his biceps and felt them tighten under my fingers, but a moment later, he said, "Bro, you're early."

I peeked around Alex to find someone stepping forward, a young blond man wearing a suit. I could see now he was holding a couple of bags that looked like it could be take-out food. "You actually got someone to deliver food to us? At this place?"

"This is one of my analysts, Eric," he said as the two walked toward each other. Slapping Eric on the shoulder with one hand, Alex accepted the bags with the other. "Thanks, man. I appreciate it."

"Did I have a choice?" Eric said.

Laughing, Alex replied, "No."

I stepped up to them, about to introduce myself, when Eric stuck his hand out. "Hey, Ava, nice to meet you."

I couldn't hide my surprise so I just shook my head, grinned, and said, "You too. And thanks for doing this." I wasn't sure what kind of situation this was or how Alex had somehow coerced this young up-and-comer to drive all the way here, but I didn't know much about his business either.

"So, you're not worried about Eric telling people about us?" I said after he'd left, a hand on my hip.

Alex scoffed. "He knows I'd beat his ass." When I shot him a look, he corrected with, "In the figurative sense, of course."

I pointed to the food. "Let me guess, burgers?"

"Do you even know me?" he said, lifting his brows.

Twenty minutes later we were sitting on the floor amongst poofy pillows, finishing the last remnants of my favorite dish, Vietnamese fajitas, cartons, plates and napkins scattered across the coffee table.

"I'm just going to say it... That was one of the best dinners I've had in a long time." I leaned up against the front edge of the couch, where Alex had his long arm draped across the cushion. He closed his hand around my shoulder, the small gesture making me so content. I turned my face up to him, letting my smile show. "I'm impressed..."

"To be honest, I can't believe it all came off without a hitch."

"You went to a lot of trouble, and I appreciate it." I brushed my lips up the column of his neck.

"Well, you did challenge me," he said against my hair.

"See what you can do with a little motivation," I teased.

As punishment, he slid his hand under my armpit and

pinched my side, making me squirm. But he also tightened his hold on me so I couldn't get away.

I squealed "Stop" through my laughter.

He pulled me halfway on top of him, the hard ridges of his chest so inviting. He brushed his open mouth over mine as my giggles died. We kissed for a few moments, his hands running along my back, before he suddenly repositioned us so I was with my back against the pillows and he was lying against my side.

"Do you know how long I've dreamt of this?" he asked, delivering feather-light kisses to my mouth, my cheek, my neck. His hand teased the edge of my blouse, sending chills over my whole body. It only took moments of Alex painting me with his lips before I was panting with need, but my rational brain was fighting for attention, too. Before my voice of reason could step in, however, Alex pulled back and gazed down at me.

"God, you're beautiful, Ava. I don't think I've ever said that to you."

"You haven't," I said in barely a whisper. "Well...not like that, anyway."

"I'm sorry. I just... I couldn't ever let myself go there. It was better for both of us." He brushed a lock of hair away from my eye. "Now...I can't take my eyes off you."

That stole my breath away. If he kept talking like that,

I wasn't sure I could stick to this whole taking it slow thing. Still, I found myself starting, "Alex..."

He grinned and ran a thumb over my bottom lip, his eyes pinning me like he hadn't just eaten an entire meal, and I was dinner. Bending down, he kissed me once, softly, "Ava..." Then he laughed. "Give me some credit, huh?"

I narrowed my eyes at him. "What?"

"I know what you were going to say." He propped himself on an elbow to gaze down at me. "What, did you actually think I was going to make our first time together be in some old abandoned building? I'd hope you would give me more credit than that."

"Well you did transform it into a little bit of paradise with these blankets and fluffy pillows but... I don't know." I shrugged, uncertain what else to say.

Alex took my hand and laced our fingers together. "Ava, I did not bring you here so we could have sex. And if I really wanted to impress you, and get you in my bed at the same time, I would've taken you to a five-star hotel and gotten us a suite."

I perked up at the idea, unable to hide my interest or my smile.

"Ah, come on!" He collapsed back onto the pillows so we were side by side, but he still held my hand.

"I'm sorry, this is way better," I said, giggling. "Continue."

"I wanted somewhere where we could spend time together... not worry about being seen by anyone, and alleviate some of your anxiety over us sleeping together." He brought my hand to his mouth and kissed my knuckles.

Taking my hand away, I lifted up and leaned on his chest, saying, "Hey. First of all, I don't have *anxiety* over sleeping together."

When he didn't seem convinced, I added, "I have thoughts and maybe *concerns*, but definitely not anxiety. I would say it's more...excitement." To prove my point, I leaned over and kissed him. Then I unbuttoned the top button of his dress shirt and slipped my hand inside, smoothing it across his chest as we kissed.

"You're playing with fire, little girl."

"So...what do we do now?"

My hair fell across his cheek, and he tugged at a piece of it. "Spend as much time together as we can."

Without a word, I moved his shirt aside, so I could rest my cheek on his bare chest, a small consolation.

"I don't just want you, Ava," he said, stroking the back of my head. "I want you in my life."

"I want that too. And I hope that means we can share every part of ourselves." I ran my finger over the scar on the left side of his chest. I knew how he'd gotten it but only minimal details, and he'd never wanted to discuss it.

There was a long pause before he said, "You know that part, too..."

"Not all of it. And not how you feel about it now." I hesitated. "About her... You never want to talk about it."

"I still don't."

We were quiet for a long time after that, and as I fought against my heavy lids, so safe and relaxed against his solid frame, I heard him say just as I drifted off, "Maybe someday..."

Chapter Fifteen

Ava

Two years ago

The midday sun shined down on the mahogany casket as friends and family lined up to place a single rose on top of its hard surface. Alex was the last one to say a final goodbye to his father, a man some called a callous businessman but few realized he was just as callous as a father. Most had simply respected the man for the decisions he had to make for his son, even if he did abuse his power. In the end, he was only trying to protect his boy from a mother who couldn't even take care of herself. Sadly, it was like Alex had lost two parents on that fateful day because his dad turned cold and distant. Alex had wanted more than anything to have the man present in his life. When he turned eighteen, the distance between them only grew. Now it was too late.

After the final prayer was said, I kept my eyes trained on Alex. He'd yet to show any emotion, and his stoic demeanor concerned me. The others might not have sensed it, but whenever his eyes shot to me, I saw all the pain and loneliness he kept at bay.

When the mourners began to disperse, Sammy and I hung back to wait for Alex and make sure he was all right. Most everyone made their way to the Bannister house for the repast, which my parents took the lead on. They'd been amazing through all this and loved Alex so much.

When Sammy said he'd drive Alex back, Mark came up to me and asked if I was ready. "Can you get the car and pull up?" I asked, eyeing the woman I'd seen earlier, hiding in the shadows. I wasn't totally certain if it was her, but since she was still lurking around, I had to know. We moved toward each other, and in an instant, I knew not only that it was Alex's mom but that she'd wanted to speak with me. I had seen photos of her and heard the stories about her addiction and what she had done when Alex was just a boy, so I was a little guarded when we finally reached each other.

"You're Ava." She was probably close to five-nine, dirty-blond hair, her face weathered but features pleasant, as if she'd been a stunner at one point, but her lifestyle tainted her looks. She darted her eyes around, and I figured she was making sure Alex didn't see her. She'd been absent from his life, partially because of Alex's father —or so I assumed. I didn't know all the details, only that Alex's dad never wanted her to have contact.

"I am. Hi, Maggie." I gave her a small grin, thinking just maybe I could do something to help make this tragedy less painful for Alex.

"You live in Las Vegas, right?"

"I do."

"I, uh, saw you."

"What?" Suddenly, I felt uncomfortable with this stranger, and I wasn't sure how she knew where I lived or why she was asking. I darted my eyes around to see if anyone was close by.

"I'm sorry, it's not what you think." She shook her head. "I know all about you and Sammy, your parents...I appreciate you all so much and how you've cared for my boy over the years."

I could hear the pain in her voice when she used the words *my boy*. I couldn't fault her for wanting to know something about his life. "We all love him."

"I know..." She nodded. "I've seen some pictures...on social media." Then she rushed to say, "Just to see parts of his life, you know. Anyway, I moved to Vegas about a year ago and saw the pictures of you in that show, so I went."

She smiled but it was sad. "You were amazing, by the way."

I felt weird saying it, but I thanked her.

"Anyway, I was hoping maybe we could get together some time...talk." She clutched her purse as it hung off her shoulder, as if this were incredibly important.

"I don't know..." Alex didn't even want us to bring up her name. How would he feel about this? I couldn't imagine how much she was suffering, but I had to think of Alex.

"I know what you must think of me..."

She held my gaze and I had to respect that. "I don't even know you." It was the truth and an easy way to avoid the obvious.

"I did some terrible things, and I know Alex hates me, but..." Her gaze darted around, this time not to watch for anyone seeing her, but to avoid me seeing her eyes fill with liquid. "I don't even know why I'm here."

"You love your son," I said softly.

Pulling a tissue from her purse, she said, "I do. I always have. I never meant to hurt him..." As she dabbed at her eyes, her hand trembled.

I sighed. "Look, I'm not sure this would be okay with Alex, me talking to you. He doesn't talk about you... I don't know all the details of why you couldn't be in his life when he was younger, but what about when he became an adult? Why didn't you try to be a part of his life then?"

She shook her head, dabbed her eyes again. "It's not an easy answer. And one that would take more time than you have. That's why I wondered if..." Almost as if she'd decided the answer would be no, she steeled herself, stuffed her tissue into the side pocket of her purse. "Never mind. Thank you for taking a moment."

She turned to leave, and I called her name. When she looked back at me, I said, "I volunteer at the Caring Hands food pantry Wednesday mornings."

She showed me a slim smile, gave a nod, and walked off.

When Mark and I arrived at Alex's dad's house, guilt sat in my stomach. Obviously, I wasn't going to mention talking to his mother today, but at some point he needed to know. Inside, the house was crowded, mostly people Mark had never met, so when he saw my dad out back drinking a beer, he asked, "Hey, mind if I go talk to your dad?"

Wanting to find Alex, I said, "Yeah, I'll meet you out there. Just going to say hi to a few people." More guilt. Mark didn't know how close Alex and I were, and I could never explain our relationship, especially since I didn't understand it myself.

I moved through the different groups of friends and family, my eyes scanning only for him. My chest tightened, and I felt a sting at the back of my eyes. It was almost as if Alex's pain had permeated my own being. He'd always been a part of our family, but losing his dad, knowing he had no relationship with his mother, must have made him feel so alone in this world.

About to check the kitchen, I caught sight of Alex heading upstairs, and I followed him. He hadn't made it as far as his old bedroom. Instead, he was standing in the hallway, looking at some pictures hanging on the wall.

"How are you holding up?" It was all I could think to say, but it sounded lame to my own ears. I put my hand on his back and felt him tense.

Alex was quiet for long moments, then said, "I think this was the only time he was proud of me." He gestured with his head to a baseball team photo.

"Was that CIF championship?" I grinned, seeing a young Alex so happy in the moment.

He nodded.

"I think you're wrong. Maybe your father wasn't the most demonstrative person, but he loved you, and he was proud of you." My words felt useless because the truth was, Alex needed his father's love. He needed it to make up for not having his mother. It wasn't the time to point out the fact that my parents had done all they could to make up for that.

When he only shook his head, I took a chance and

moved in between him and the photos. "What can I do, Alex?"

"Nothing. There's nothing anyone can do. You can go back to Mark now."

Ignoring his words and his cold tone, I said, "I'm not leaving you."

His jaw clenched as he finally looked me in the eye. "Ava... Don't, okay?" His breathing grew heavy, but I didn't back down. "I don't want to do this. I—can't. This is part of life, and I'll get through it."

His last words, delivered so robotically, broke my heart, but I still didn't budge. If there was anyone in his life that made him vulnerable, I knew it was me. He put up even more of a front with Sammy. "I'm here," I whispered, fighting back my own tears.

Alex grabbed me by my arms in a firm grip, his face twisted in anger and pain, and I hoped I wasn't making a mistake, forcing him to address these feelings. "Dammit, Ava..." Then he pulled me into his arms, tucked his head into the crook of my neck, and sobbed as I held him tightly.

Chapter Sixteen

Alex

Present Day

When I walked into the house that was my second home for as long as I could remember, I felt an unexpected hesitation. Sue and Denny had given me a key in high school and firmly told me they better not ever answer the door to me again. But now that Ava was there...and her buddy Gunnar...I almost worried I'd see something that wouldn't sit well with me.

And that was exactly what happened. The soft music playing should have been my first clue. *What the actual fuck is going on here?* Okay, it took me a second to figure it out, but that didn't mean I wanted to see a shirtless Gunnar lying on his back, his tanned pecs glistening as he held Ava up by her ankles while she balanced herself holding his ankles. They were like human goddamn bunkbeds! If I wasn't instantly annoyed by the scene, I might have been impressed by their form and strength, two straight-as-arrows fit bodies holding a push-up pose.

Thankfully, they hadn't noticed me, which gave me time to pull my more rational self into place. Because the last time I saw someone touching Ava, I'd overreacted; that would only piss her off.

They're just friends, I reminded myself. And apparently doing couples yoga. And touching each other. *Lucky bastard!* I took a few deep breaths and belted out, "Honey, I'm home!"

They both turned their heads in my direction, still frozen in their poses.

"Alex?" The way Ava said it told me she was not expecting me.

"Hey, bro," Gunnar said with a smirk. The word *bro* sounded foreign coming from his mouth. Gunnar slowly lowered his arms until Ava's lower half was resting on top of him, so she had no choice but to do the same. Those few seconds before she rolled off him, their bodies pressed together, felt like someone ripping a hangnail off of my thumb, while Gunnar clearly enjoyed the whole scene.

Popping quickly to her feet, Ava said in a panicked tone, "What are you doing here?" She darted her eyes toward the kitchen where her mother likely was—if the delicious smell of garlic bread was any indication.

"I'm here for dinner," I said, holding up the bottle of wine I'd brought.

She mouthed the word *fuck*, and I tried not to take it personally.

Gunnar came up behind her. "We're glad you're here, aren't we, Ava honey?"

I rolled my eyes, but before either of us could respond, Gunnar said, "Well, I'm going to hit the shower." He got two steps before, he shot a look over his shoulder. "Unless anyone wants to join me..."

Ava and I both glared at him.

"I'm kidding. Geez." As he walked down the hall, I heard him mumble, "Someone needs to get some."

When Ava turned back to me, I lifted my brows, as if to say I could accommodate that request for her.

Her response was to shoot a look over her shoulder. "Why didn't you tell me you were coming?"

"I suppose since you live here, I figured you knew. I come for dinner the last Saturday of every month, but because of game night, I missed."

"I should have known something was up. Mom never makes manicotti. Says it's too much work."

I showed her a half grin, proud of my special treatment. "I guess I'm worth it. Now if you'll excuse me..." I moved past her but not before giving her ass a little smack. Those tight yoga pants were irresistible. I was sure her mouth was hanging open, so I didn't need to look back, just continued on to the kitchen. Business as usual.

Sue greeted me with a giant hug, then took the wine from my hand. "How are you, sweetie?" she said, patting me on the shoulder with her free hand.

"Good. Busy."

She flipped the light switch on the oven and peeked in, replying, "Grab yourself something to drink, then you can give me a real answer."

"What do you mean?" I chuckled and pulled a beer from the fridge. Popping it open, I quickly added, "Sammy and Cass coming?" hoping that would distract her. Sue was like a drug-sniffing dog at the border.

"Dax has an ear infection. And you know what I mean." She leaned against the counter. "I know what the one-word answers mean. Are you dating someone? Is that it?" She grinned as if she hoped that was it. Too bad the truth would wipe that smile right off her face.

"I'll be closing that Brilliance deal I told you about..." I took a long pull from my beer. "How long before we eat?" I hadn't thought about facing Sue, keeping this from her. I knew I would have to, but I didn't realize how hard it would be.

Sue shot me that disapproving mom look. "Uh-huh. I

see. I suppose you'll tell me about her when you're ready." She pulled a stack of dishes off the counter and pushed it out to me as if the message were clear to set the table. "Dinner in about half an hour."

Later, when we were all seated at the table, there was an awkward vibe with Gunnar there and not Sammy and his family. Denny talked about his looming retirement, Ava filled us all in on the apartment it looked like her and Gunnar were going to get, and Sue told the story of a champion of a baby girl born at just twenty-eight weeks and, of course, she teared up as she relayed the details, even with the happy ending.

As if a switch flipped, Sue turned to Ava and said, "So, heard anything about this new girl Alex is dating?"

Ava's eyes popped wide. "What? Me? Why would I—"

"Ooh, who's the lucky lady?" Gunnar cut in. I wasn't sure if it was to save Ava or to goad me.

I dug into my cheesy pasta tube and took a big bite, occupying my mouth.

"Why are we ganging up on Alex?" Denny put in. "Leave the man alone."

I grinned, not just for the support but because he called me a man and not a boy, which had been his practice. "Thank you, Denny. Truth is my life isn't that interesting. You all know how much I work." I turned to

Sue. "That's why I appreciate these meals so much. This is amazing, by the way..."

Sue gave me a genuine smile that time. "You're welcome. And I'm sorry to give you such a hard time."

Despite her words, I knew she wouldn't let this go.

After dinner, we all pitched in to clear the table and put things away. Surprisingly, Gunnar offered to do the dishes, since Sue and Denny wanted to catch a movie. That left Ava and me to fend for ourselves. When she suggested we watch a movie, I couldn't say no. Anytime with her, being near her, just looking at her, I'd gladly take over anything else. But if I were being honest with myself, it was getting harder and harder to hold myself back. Waiting to be with her had been killing me, and the fact that I couldn't have her yet, made me want her all the more.

So, when I entered the living room and found her on the couch—having changed into some skimpy short pajama bottoms and a tank top—I almost lost my shit.

My pulse sped up as she stared up at me, a sexy grin pulling at her full mouth, her hand resting on the blanket next to her. My brain went wild with the things I could do to her under that blanket.

"Are you coming..." she said in a soft silky tone.

I looked toward the front of the house. Sue and Denny

should be gone for hours... And Gunnar, well, I'd handle him if he bothered us.

Screw it. "Oh, I'm coming all right."

Taking a seat next to Ava on the couch that I'd spent many days and nights on over the years, watching sports with Sammy was more than surreal—but in a way it felt wrong. Sure a bunch of us kids would pile in there to watch a movie, and many times Ava was there, but I never planned to feel her up on it under a blanket. Sue and Denny would likely be home close to midnight, and Ava had texted her mom a random question just to make sure everything was all right and there were no mishaps that would bring them home early. But it wasn't all about getting caught. This was their little girl—in their eyes anyway.

As she went through the guide and we debated which movie to see, we were sitting close enough our legs touched. She rested her free hand on my thigh, and I didn't know if it was done absentmindedly or not, but when she began moving it up and down, my loose-fit jeans suddenly felt snug with the blood racing through my veins. I crossed one leg over my knee, resting my ankle on it.

I wasn't sure what Ava saw happening tonight, but the longer she rubbed my thigh the more I saw myself needing an all-or-nothing scenario.

"Rom-com, action? Or thriller?" She turned her head, and her lips were inches from mine, so full and stained light pink.

"I don't care," I said shortly.

Narrowing her gaze, she said, "Since when?"

I shook my head, torn between everything I wanted and the sense of doom—however irrational—looming over my head.

Setting down the remote, she turned her body to face me. Her wavy dark hair draped over her shoulder. "What's wrong?" she said, stroking her hand across my cheek like it was the most natural thing in the world.

"This... This whole thing feels off." I glanced around the room, my eyes landing on a framed photo on the mantel of all of us at one of our trips up to Big Bear. Ava, barely a teen, looking adorable and innocent. "I don't know if I can do this with you tonight."

Instead of getting annoyed with me, she grinned, leaned in, and dragged her lips along my jaw. "You didn't have a problem the other night, on our date..."

Her bodywash floated under my nose, and all I could see was her in the shower, her skin glistening with droplets of water. "That was different," I whispered. "We weren't *here*...." When her lips found mine, I didn't fight it. I couldn't. Tucking my hand behind her neck, I held her in place so I could get my fill of her, plundering her mouth like a starved man. Instinctively, I leaned back as we kissed, pulling her with me until she was flush on top of my body, her knees straddling my lap. My hands smoothed down her back, and I stopped at her round ass, where I pressed until she moaned into my mouth.

"Holy hot cross buns!" Gunnar said from the doorway, and the two of us popped up, breathing heavily and exchanging awkward glances.

I didn't say a word because I'd either come off looking like a jackass or say something rude that would piss one of them off.

Ava pulled her tank top back into place and said, "We're...just about to watch a movie."

"Looked more like you were making one."

I shot a glare his way, but he threw up his hands and said, "Ah, shit, I just remembered I'm supposed to facetime my honey Cheryl." He waved a hand at us and walked by, adding, "Keep that volume up nice and loud now, kids. I hear any panting, and I'll come back wearing a bow and a smile." He laughed like it was the funniest thing he'd ever heard.

"I'm sorry," Ava said with a wince once he was gone.

I clenched my jaw. "And you're going to live with that guy." Somehow I had to come to terms with that. Or maybe I should just have Ava move in with me. Then I could tie her up in my bed and never let her go.

"He's not growing on you just a tiny bit?" Her brows hung in wait.

I had to be fair—at least the guy supported us. And he was fucking funny sometimes. "I don't know. Ask me again after you guys move in together."

Grinning, she said, "How about we forget all that and watch a movie?" She pulled the blanket over herself and halfway over me. "Maybe we can cuddle?"

It was an ambitious plan that was tougher than we'd both thought. Twenty minutes into the movie, I couldn't keep my hands off her. Feeling those silky thighs, which she'd draped over me, knowing only a thin pair of pajama bottoms and some panties separated me from heaven... As if my hand had a mind of its own, it caressed along her inner thigh, moving higher and higher each time.

When my fingers brushed inside her shorts, along the seam of her underwear, I heard her breathing labor, glanced over and saw the heady look in her eyes. I definitely didn't want to alert Gunnar to anything, but I had to have this small taste of Ava, bring her a little pleasure. Clearly she wanted it. Tempting fate a bit more, I continued moving my hand where I knew she craved it to be. Her chest filled and mine did too. Her mouth parted, and I closed the distance between us, connected our lips, searching with my tongue. As our kiss grew deeper, more intense, so did the movement of my hand until Ava's groans of pleasure grew so loud I drew back, smiling with pride but also to give her a warning look as I slowed my hand. She, of course, giggled but gripped my wrist to hold it in place, then leaned back in to capture my mouth.

This side of Ava was surprising and completely welcome. I brushed my lips over her mouth. "God damn, Ava..." I whispered. "Do you know how bad I want you right now?"

"I actually do," she said breathlessly. Her eyes darted to the hall. "We could go in my room?"

My girl's will power was worse than mine. "What happened to waiting?" I said with a small grin so she wouldn't think I was criticizing her. "That was your idea."

"I know, but... It literally feels like we've been waiting years for this."

I knew exactly what she meant, but I wasn't about to have our first time be under the Steadmans' roof. "Don't get me wrong. I want you... *Badly*." I ran my thumb over her bottom lip, aching to kiss it again, but another pang—something else—hit me square in the gut. "Physically, emotionally...I want it all. But, Ava, there's already been these feelings here that I don't quite know what to do with, you know? You, Sammy, your parents...I've loved you all for so long and now with you...there's all this other...stuff, and I'm not sure how I'm supposed to reconcile that."

Her gaze had held mine with every word I spoke, a

tenderness in them I wasn't sure how to take. She sighed. "You're right. I feel that too." Then she giggled. "It's just... when you touch me...pretty much all reason goes out the door."

I didn't resist then, moved in and nipped at her mouth. "Now that's my girl." My hand was still resting between her legs, unmoving. "We'll have our time..." With my lips against hers, I said, "And I'll want you to scream my name. Tonight, though... I can at least give you a little preview, but you're going to have to keep that little mouth quiet."

Chapter Seventeen

Ava

"You are such a little liar." Gunnar pulled a box off the counter and moved it to the kitchen table before hopping up on top of it to sit.

"Come on, we need to keep working," I said with a whine to my voice that I regretted. I did not want to become the mom of our apartment. Plus, whenever I'd gone to his place, it was always well-decorated, neat, and clean. "We're never going to get this shit done if we don't keep at it."

"We have forever to unpack, and those fine young men out there are still unloading the truck, so spill it before they come back."

I pulled some dish towels from a box and shoved them

into a drawer. "I don't know what you're talking about. We were watching a movie." I shrugged.

"You cannot tell me that man of yours didn't give you the massive O when you guys were on the couch under that blanket. I heard...noises."

I opened another box that wasn't labeled for some reason and found it was filled with what looked like designer shoes. "This isn't kitchen stuff," I said, annoyed.

Gunnar leaned over and peeked inside. "Yeah, those are mine."

"Why do you have a box of designer shoes? Some of these are women's shoes."

He stared at me with a smirk on his face. "I'll tell if you tell."

I threw a look over my shoulder to check we were safe. "Fine, be that way. But, I'm not gonna *say* anything because I don't want to get in the habit of kissing and telling, especially when I'm trying to get you and Alex to get along." Then, I gave him a single nod, holding back a grin.

"Holy shit! I knew it. But you guys still haven't done it yet, right?"

I threw a hand on my hip and glared at him.

"Fine...respecting privacy and all that crap." His shoulders slumped like he was twelve and I'd told him no video games.

I scoffed. "First of all, now you have to tell me where you got all these. And second, you're going to get your ass off the counter and take this box into your room."

Reversing the order, Gunnar hopped off the counter. "Before we left, I stopped by my parents' house, told them I was collecting for charity, got some stuff from their closet and my little sister's."

"And they just gave you all these shoes that look brand new?" My tone told him I was more than skeptical.

Lifting the box, he said, "*Gave* is a tricky word…"

I smacked him on the shoulder and then followed him out of the kitchen. "I can't believe you stole all these."

"My family doesn't need them and probably won't even know they're gone. Besides, I thought we could bring them with us to that homeless shelter we were going to visit when we were settled."

"Oh, good idea…I think?"

"Hey, just because they're homeless doesn't mean they don't want to look dazzling in a pair of Louboutins."

"You're right," I said as he moved into the hallway while I stopped in the living room, noticing Alex walking up with a box. "And that's why I love you…and why I put up with your crap. Now go put that box away." I rushed to pull the door open farther and then hold it for Alex.

"Did you just say you loved Gunnar?" He passed me

with a glare I could tell was forced. "While I'm over here killing myself carrying all these boxes?"

"You're fine..." I pointed to the living room. "And I'm pretty sure those are pillows so..." Then I tapped him on the ass before I realized how dumb that was.

Because a second later, my brother, Sammy, was coming through the door, carrying an artificial plant in a basket. "All that's left are those two floor lamps."

"Thank you both so much." I glanced around the room at all the boxes, the thought of all the work ahead not as terrible as I'd anticipated. I was just happy to be out of my parents' house. They were awesome about all this, but now I could have time with Alex and not stress over it.

"I'll grab those lamps," Alex said.

But just as he rounded the couch, Gunnar came from the hallway. "Wings and beers on me." He held up his phone. "There's a place not far from here that's supposed to be amazing. Nice bar. Great food."

"I could eat," Sammy said. "Thanks."

"Um, hello? Don't you have a wife and child to get to?" I chimed in.

"Yeah, Alex, don't-cha?" Sammy chuckled.

"Hey!" I said in defense of my sister-in-law and nephew.

"Come on, I'm kidding. They're at Sadie's place, so I would have been on my own for dinner anyway."

Gunnar moved farther into the living room. "How about you, big guy?" he said to Alex, gripping his shoulder.

I caught a wince from Alex, but he still said, "Sure, why not?"

We took a few minutes to make sure everything was in and secure, locked up our new apartment, and then headed over to Ted's Tavern, arriving in the thick of happy hour.

I sat between Alex and Gunnar at the table, across from Sammy, which was good and bad. I didn't have to worry about avoiding weird eye contact with Alex, but Sammy had the perfect view to catch anything suspect between Alex and me.

As it turned out, we were all starved, and the wings were amazing. Most of the conversation was around Gunnar and his family. Alex and Sammy were giving him the third degree like they would if he were a date or boyfriend, and I pretty much let it happen. I knew Gunnar could hold his own. But then the guys turned up the heat.

"So, you just gonna live off your trust fund, or you're actually going to work?" Alex said.

My mouth flew open. "Alex!"

"It's totally fine," Gunnar said, putting a hand on my arm.

Sammy leaned in, elbows on the table as if he were dying to know the answer too.

"I do have some skills," Gunnar said, passing his gaze around the table.

"That's right. He's an incredible dancer, extremely smart, and has better people skills than either of you."

"Thanks, baby... And actually it's those people skills I'll tap into. I have a lot of experience working in my family's hotels in Vegas. I'll probably use some of my hookups and try to get a concierge job. If there's one thing I'm the freaking best at, it's planning fun shit to do and spreading joy."

"I gotta hand it to you, man," Sammy said. "You're using what you learned from your family but not so much their money."

"Thank you, sir," Gunnar said like he was talking to his prom date's dad.

I elbowed Alex in the side, and he flinched.

"Yeah, yeah, respectable."

Gunnar gave him the side-eye before he continued, "Full disclosure, though, I've enjoyed the benefits of their wealth for a long-ass time."

"But you do a lot of giving back and charity work, and that counts too." I nodded emphatically.

"And don't you two worry... I'm going to take real good

care of your little girl." Gunnar draped an arm around me, and I couldn't help but bust out laughing.

I didn't care that they were all talking about me like I wasn't there. I knew I could stand on my own two feet, but I was grateful I had three amazing men who looked out for me.

Alex pushed out his chair. "Well, I'm going to the bar to get drinks. Our server is MIA."

"I'll help!" Gunnar said excitedly, jumping up to follow Alex. He threw a grin at me over his shoulder. Gunnar might put up this silly front, but I knew he sought their approval.

I watched them make their way up there and noticed it was pretty crowded at the bar area too. As they were waiting for a space to open up, a gorgeous and tall blond ran up to Alex and threw her arms around him. They were almost the same height, and I wondered if she was some model he'd dated. My pulse quickened as I waited for him to give her the brush off, but instead his arms went to her back. And then, she kissed him on his fucking mouth!

Chapter Eighteen

Ava

My heart lodged in my throat as I watched Alex in a lip lock with some other woman. The logical side of my mind immediately jumped in. *You guys never specifically discussed being exclusive.* But then the emotional side bitch-slapped logic. *Bullshit, we were exclusive the moment we kissed.* It was unspoken but no less real. Plus, there was that Jessica incident, and he assured me I was the only one he wanted.

I felt the sting of tears threaten my eyes, and it sent a current of panic through me. Of course I didn't want Alex to see me crying over him, but more importantly, Sammy, who had been sitting across from me, was now next to me and seeing the same thing I was. He'd know about Alex and me if he saw how upset this made me.

Gunnar had been trying to navigate an opening to the bar so he didn't see the kiss. A small relief.

I reached for my water just as the two of them pulled apart. Watching them over my glass, I studied their mouths, wishing I could make out what they were saying.

"Mom says Alex is seeing someone," Sammy said, leaning in. "I wonder if that's her and why the hell he didn't tell me."

I shrugged, steeling myself. "Who knows... Who freaking cares." I internally winced at that last part, hearing a twinge of hostility in my tone.

"Hey...we've never really talked about it, but I know you've sort of had a crush on Alex all these years."

I whipped my head around to face him. "Shut up. I never had a *crush* on Alex." Wow, defensive much?

"Okay, liar."

Why is everyone saying that to me today? I held his gaze, hoping he couldn't see the truth.

"Look, I don't care, and I get it. It's not like every girl I've ever known hasn't had a crush on Alex, but you're my sister, and now that you're living here again, well, I hope you meet someone..." The "else" was conveniently left off.

"Right now I'm just worrying about getting settled and

figuring out what I want to do with my life." Not totally a lie, but it still tasted off.

He sighed. "You'll get there, little sis." Then, just when I thought he'd let it drop, he added, "It's probably good that you and Alex never got together, though."

"Why do you say that?" I couldn't help but ask.

"I just don't think he's the commitment type." I glanced at him then, and he head-gestured over to Alex. "You know what I mean?"

Alex appeared nervous now, still talking to the blond woman, but I caught his eyes darting in our direction. Anger and frustration built back up in me—at Alex and at Sammy. Once again, I couldn't let it go, saying, "People do change."

"He's my best friend, but I don't know... I love the guy, but there's some issues there. We both know. And he won't talk to me..."

"His mom..." I said it under my breath, the thing that could tear Alex and me apart.

"Yeah... His parents did a number on him."

I couldn't stand listening to any of it any longer. "I need to use the restroom." I pushed from my chair and caught Alex's gaze. Maybe I was imagining it, but I thought I saw guilt and frustration in his eyes. Darting mine away, I headed to the back of the bar, my heart racing for more than one reason. As mad as I was at Alex, my heart broke for him whenever the topic of his parents came up. That was another scary thought I wasn't ready to face. My feelings for the man. He'd had my heart for so long it was like our relationship fast forwarded, even though it had only started.

I entered the bathroom and went right to the sink to see if I looked all right. My eyes were a little red, but that wasn't uncommon in a bar. I snatched a paper towel and dabbed at one eye, swallowing back a lump in my throat. I dreaded going back out there, facing Alex, acting like everything was fine.

The door popped open as I dabbed my other eye one last time, and in the mirror I locked eyes with "the blonde." As if she were in there specifically for me, she came up right beside me. "Hey... Got something in your eye?"

Taking a slight pause, I replied, "Yeah, wing sauce I think. Didn't realize when I touched my eye." I tried to manage a smile, but just the sight of her flawless skin and huge blue eyes, picturing her plump lips on Alex's, set my skin on fire.

"Look, Ava..."

My mouth flew open. "How do you know my name?"

She tilted her head with her brows raised, as if the answer were obvious. "I'm Lauren, by the way."

Tossing the paper towel into the trash, I said, "Nice to

meet you." Then I moved to the door, but her words stopped me.

"That kiss was nothing..."

I turned a glare on her. "Excuse me?"

"Please don't be upset with Alex." Genuine remorse showed on her face.

I shook my head. "Alex can do whatever he pleases."

"This was my fault. The guy's crazy about you, and I just want—"

"Wait, what?" Stepping back over to her, I continued, "Why do you know about me and if you do, why the hell would you kiss Alex?" I folded my arms over my chest.

When she sighed, I figured out part of the story. "You guys dated, right?"

"Dated? No. We had one date, and he talked about you the whole time."

I couldn't hold back the small grin that formed on my face.

Lauren closed the distance between us, then surprised me by touching my arm. "And the only reason I kissed him was because some creepy dude kept hitting on me, and it was really making me nervous. I saw Alex and just... reacted. But it worked. I hope you understand."

With a nod, I said, "I do." My whole body relaxed then. "Thank you for coming and telling me."

She gave me a single nod. "Well, I've gotta run..."

Her sweet smile made me feel a little guilty for how I reacted, but all I could think to say was, "Bye."

Sammy left pretty soon after I emerged from the bathroom and Alex, Gunnar, and I didn't address the elephant in the room as we drank our beers. I almost felt bad for Alex as he watched me carefully and seemed to examine my every move, as if I were a difficult puzzle to solve.

When we walked to our cars, Alex took my hand, saying, "I need to talk to you" before dragging me over to his Mercedes.

I let him pull me, holding up a finger to Gunnar, who shouted back sarcastically, "Sure, I don't mind sitting around waiting..."

I thought about making him squirm, but we didn't have time or room in this relationship for playing games, especially when we couldn't be free to be together. "Alex, it's okay..."

As if I hadn't said a word, he gripped the back of my head and pinned me with a desperate glare. "That wasn't me, Ava. Lauren, she—"

Reaching up on my toes, I pressed my mouth to his. I'd meant it to be a reassuring, sweet kiss, but Alex turned it into something fierce, pulling me hard against his body and pouring out his pent-up frustration on me. The result was my blood pumping overtime and my body heating at his relentless need for me.

We pulled away, both breathless, but kept our faces only inches apart. He dipped his forehead against mine and before he could say anything, I said, "Lauren found me in the bathroom, told me what happened."

Nipping at my lip he said, "I can't stand this...being away from you, not being able to hold you, reassure you when I need to."

"I know," I whispered.

"That's why I'm taking you away. We need to get out of this town and spend some time together. Alone."

Chapter Nineteen

Alex

*N*ot the most romantic choice for a getaway, but it turned out Vegas made the most sense for Ava and I to go to. That way she could tell her parents she was going to meet with her office, visit friends, and see one of her friend's shows, which was mostly true. And given how close Sin City was, I didn't think any of the Steadmans would even know I was gone.

My hand had been nestled between Ava's shapely thighs for the last hour of the drive as we played Who Knows Who Better. The whole thing started when she'd tried to tell me that I didn't like pizza the way most people liked pizza. And she'd actually convinced me she was right, giving several examples. Basically, I could take it or leave it. Then I'd clapped back with how she wasn't attracted to male dancer bodies despite being a dancer. I was particularly proud of proving that one, given one male dancer she was living with.

"What about pets?" she said after a few minutes of just the sound of the car and radio playing.

I didn't turn my head, but I also didn't hide my grin as I moved my hand a little higher between her legs, brushing my thumb over her inner thigh, which was exposed from her short shorts. "You sure you want to go there right now? I wouldn't want to get us in an accident."

Pushing my hand lower, she said, "I didn't mean that."

We were both laughing, but my body was on fire at the visual and the thought of a hotel room in our very near future. I glanced at the clock. With dinner reservations and the show commitment, we'd have less than an hour to check in and get ready. That wasn't enough time in my book for what I'd had planned for Ava. I'd just have to tough it out until the end of the night. Something that was getting harder and harder. *Literally*.

When we finally made it to the hotel and up to our room on the eighteenth floor, Ava went right to the window. "I always love this view. Kinda reminds me of being on stage with all the lights."

I pressed up behind her and nuzzled her neck. "I

wouldn't mind seeing you on stage again." She was so damn beautiful up there.

Turning her head to the side, she whispered, "Who says I can't dance just for you?"

"*Fuck...*" I'd meant to only think it, but somehow it came out. I captured her mouth with mine and gripped her neck, holding her in place to deepen the kiss. After a moment, she spun and rose up on her toes to wrap her arms around my neck, sighing in that sweet tune before I dove back in for her mouth.

All I had to do was back her up a few steps and the bed was right there. Tempting for more reasons than I could count. It was like this moment was fifteen years in the making, and I wasn't sure how I could wait another second, especially with the feel of her soft curves pressed against me, the heat of the kiss, her heady little moans... On instinct, I suppose, I took those few steps, guided her back toward the bed.

But before I could ease her down onto the mattress, Ava pulled back. "Wow, um..." She laughed, her face a gorgeous pink hue. "I was just thinking..."

"That we should just stay in tonight?" I gave her a squinty smile, running my hands down her back to the top of her ass.

"As much as that sounds"—she slid her palms to my chest, a slight press that felt like a warning—"tempting..."

"You promised Erin." One of Ava's dance buddies left tickets for us for the early show, and I wasn't going to be one of those guys that alienated his woman from her friends. "We should go." I kissed her forehead. "Plus...I'm going to need much more time than we have now." I winked and released her. "I'm going to need to take my time with you, Ava," I said, throwing a look over my shoulder to catch her eyes wide.

The little huff of air she let out was an added bonus for me as she grabbed her bag and scurried into the bathroom.

Erin's show was one of those acrobatic/dance shows with a crap-ton of lights and something happening in every part of the stage. But what was more entertaining for me was after, when we went backstage, and I got to see Ava in her element. In my eyes, Ava was everything. The total package. But to watch her peers look at her, interact with her, it really hit home how special she was, and that filled me with a sense of pride I probably didn't deserve.

The dancers had another show to get ready for, so thankfully, we didn't stay long.

Next we headed over to The Forum Shops at Caesars because Ava wanted to shop before our dinner reservations at Nobu. Never letting go of her hand, I followed her to her favorite stores, taking note of every single thing that caught her eye. Something about the domestic feel of this scenario made me blissfully content—sure, the thought of what awaited me tonight helped, but just being with Ava felt so good.

Until we stepped out of a store and almost ran into someone I didn't recognize for a split second—if it weren't for those eyes that appeared in my nightmares... We stared at each other in shocked silence for what felt like long seconds, my heart lodging in my throat. I was only barely aware I was still holding Ava's hand, when I felt it tense in mine.

My mother sputtered, "A-Alex..."

I shook my head, then pushed past her, hearing her call, "Alex, please, wait."

Ava stopped short, our hands pulling apart. "Alex, wait."

I turned back and stared at Ava, my mother's blurry form behind her.

Ava stepped toward me, took my hand again. "Can't you just—"

"No, I can't," I said matter-of-factly, darting my eyes for a beat to the woman who was basically a stranger to me, my pulse pounding and my anger building. "Come on." My legs got me moving, but it felt like I couldn't get us out of there fast enough.

Ava stayed quiet, even when we passed Nobu, and I headed to the exit. As we stepped up to the cab stand, I couldn't even meet her gaze. I couldn't think straight, didn't know if I should be ashamed for how I acted or pissed that Ava didn't back me up. Of course, I didn't even know if she knew the whole story of what happened that day. So, when she moved in front of me, and I was forced to look at her, I blurted out, "You don't understand. That woman tried to kill me."

Ava's jaw went slack as she registered what I'd just said to her. I knew it wasn't fair to drop that bombshell on her, but at the same time she had to know. It was finally time to get this out. She and Sammy only knew part of the story, and even though the memory was so vivid it was like it happened yesterday, I just never could put words to it, never wanted to acknowledge it by sharing what happened that day.

Ava slipped her hand into mine, and I could see her eyes water; it was so like her to take on the pain of someone she loved. When a cab pulled to a stop in front of us, she touched my face and said, "Let's go back to the room and talk."

We exchanged no words as we sat there, driving by happy families on vacation, young men and women dressed to the nines, ready to party like they didn't have a care in the world. All the while, Ava held my hand tightly in her lap, as if she needed me to know she was there for me.

Back in the room, I sat on the bed, and she sat next to me. Before I could say anything, she turned her body to face me and ran a hand down my back. "I'm so sorry you're hurting. You don't have to tell me anything you don't want to...but I'm ready to hear all of it."

I nodded. "I know you and Sammy have wondered what exactly happened with my mother all those years ago." I averted her gaze and shook my head, pointed my stare toward the window. "But you were around my father. You heard his comments about her. You know he kept her out of my life because she was a drug addict and never even wanted to be a mother." I felt my own eyes burn at the thought my mom hadn't wanted me. I drew in a deep breath and pressed on. "There was so much more than that, though."

I felt her forehead press against my shoulder. "Oh, Alex, that must've been so hard for you."

I forced myself to look at her. "Most of the time, I just live my life and don't think about her. But when she pops into my head, I force her out...because the last time I was with her, it was one of the worst days of my life."

Alex
Five years old...

I could barely make my legs move fast enough to keep up with my mom as she pulled me down the hall of my school. When she glanced back at me, she smiled, but I could tell she didn't mean it. Her eyes were red again, and she just kept telling me to hurry.

Once we were in the car and we pulled away from the school, I heard the beeping in the front seat. My dad had made her carry a pager and a phone so he could keep track of her.

"Is that daddy?" I asked.

She didn't answer, and when we missed the turn to our house, I said, "Mommy where are we going? Do I have a doctor's appointment?" That was what they had told me when they took me out of class.

She glanced at me in the mirror. "No, baby. We're going somewhere else, and it's a surprise."

"Is Daddy coming?" I didn't like going places without my dad, even though he sometimes wasn't nice to me or my mom. Even when she was sick or had trouble moving around, he would get mad. But I didn't think I was strong enough to help her.

"No, Daddy can't come."

I noticed she was driving pretty fast, passing other cars, and I was scared. "Will we be home in time for dinner?" Dad had said he was bringing home pizza.

"Stop asking me so many questions." She moved so I

could see more of her face in the mirror. "We have to go away, honey."

"Go away? From Daddy?" I'd heard them arguing many times before, both of them saying they were going to take me away somewhere, but they never did.

The beeping went off again, and I saw my mom pick up the pager from the seat next to her and then throw it to the ground. "Damn him. He's not taking my son away from me." She was crying, and the car was swerving some.

"Mommy, I'm scared. I want to go home." I tried not to cry, even though Dad wasn't there, but I didn't want to get in trouble. He was always grumpy when I cried.

The car jerked to the side, and I heard a horn honk. Dad always asked me questions about my mom, and if he asked about this, I knew he'd be mad. Sometimes, Mom said, "Don't tell Daddy," and I bet she would say that about this too.

I didn't know how long we drove like that, but my mom stopped answering me. It was like she was in a race, and she kept looking in the mirror.

I was watching her eyes in the mirror, so I didn't know what happened—only that suddenly the car was jerking in all directions, my body being pushed and pulled, and I heard a loud screeching noise, then smashing and crunching. My mom screamed, and so did I. I squeezed my eyes shut until everything went still.

When I opened my eyes, I knew something very bad had happened because I was on my side and had slipped out of my seatbelt some. "Mommy!" She didn't answer. "Mommy! The car is upside down!"

I couldn't help it. I started crying. After a while, I heard my mom's voice.

"Alex, get out!" She just kept screaming it over and over until I got myself moving.

I was able to crawl and climb my way out through the front where the windshield used to be, but when I got out, I didn't see my mom. She was still in the car. I was on my hands and knees on the ground. I turned back around and saw her pressed up against her door in a weird, crumpled way. I called out, "Mommy, get out."

"I can't, baby. I'm stuck. We'll have to wait for help."

I wasn't sure where we were, but I didn't see anyone around. "Wait, I hear sirens." But then I saw something else, the most horrible thing I'd ever seen. Our car had flames on it. "Mommy, the car's on fire."

"Oh, God. It's okay, just back away, sweetie, as far as you can."

I didn't listen to her. Instead, I crawled closer and peered at her through the opening I'd come out of.

"God dammit, Alex, go back. Now."

"No, Mommy, I have to help you."

"It's just my seatbelt. I can't get out of it. Someone is

coming to help. You have to stay back." She shook her head as I stared at her, tears streaming down her face.

"I don't want you to get burned, Mommy."

"Oh, my God, no. Alex, please go back."

I didn't care what she said. I crawled back through the opening and didn't notice a piece of glass sticking out until it scraped across my chest. "Mommy!" It hurt so bad.

"Dammit, Alex, why aren't you listening? What happened?"

"Please, just get out, Mommy." I reached over and tugged on her arm, but she yanked it free.

"Okay, listen," she said, breathing hard. "See if you can get a big piece of glass, and I'll try to cut the seatbelt."

I crawled around, searching, feeling the sting of pain in my chest and my hands and knees. "All the pieces are so small." I kept looking and then, I saw it. "Daddy's pocket knife!" I snatched it up and handed it to my mom.

As she started cutting, she kept telling me to get out, but I couldn't move. I was frozen, watching her sawing at the belt. The next thing I knew, hands grabbed my arms and pulled me back out of the car.

Chapter Twenty

Alex

Present Day

Ava wrapped her arms around me, held me tightly for several minutes. I wasn't sure what she would say about the story I'd just told her—I could only imagine—but at one point guilt filled my gut, and I stroked her hair. It was a lot to lay down on someone, especially someone who cared about you.

Just when I thought she might not say anything at all, she pulled back and took my hands into hers.

"Oh my God, Alex," she whispered but couldn't quite meet my eye.

A tear streamed down her cheek, and I pulled one hand from her grip to wipe it away. "I'm okay now. Please don't cry." I brushed the hair out of her face and gave her a slim smile. "I just needed to tell you."

She drew in a shaky breath and nodded. "I'm glad you did. I'm sorry I have to ask this but...are you saying that your mom was trying to kidnap you when that accident happened?"

I nodded. "I mean no one really knows exactly what my mother had planned, or what she would have actually done if we hadn't gotten in the accident."

As if she'd had a stake in the good name of my mother, she said, "She loved you. It was a terrible, terrible, thing, but maybe she would have realized it was wrong and brought you home."

It was just like her to see the good in people, but that had never been me...thanks to both my parents. "I guess we'll never know. Even if I ever spoke to her again, I could never be sure she wasn't lying."

"I don't understand. Did she go to jail? Is that why she wasn't in your life?"

"No, that was all my dad. He had all the power. Money, contacts, the best lawyers. But he also knew how California law favored the mother. Sure he could have pressed charges, but he wanted to make sure she never came back again..." I let out a shuttered sigh. Clearly I hadn't thought this out, hadn't realized how deep into this conversation I'd have to go.

"What did he do?" she asked hesitantly.

I stood then, made my way over to the window and gazed out at the Las Vegas strip. For all my mother's faults, she wasn't the only shitty parent. "Dad covered up the accident. Told me never to talk about it again. He made her sign away all rights to me, and then had her committed to a rehab program somewhere out of state."

"That had to be a horrible time for you. So confusing."

"Dad never gave me the details. Just told me she was leaving. Going away to get better. I only found out what he'd done after he died, and I went through all his paperwork."

I heard her get up from the bed. "Oh, Alex. Why didn't you tell us...Sammy at least?" She wrapped her arms around my waist, pressed her cheek to my back. For some reason that small gesture, the feel of her, knowing what it meant...it was the first time in a long time I got choked up, felt the sting of tears threaten behind my eyes. I'd made it through that whole damn story and a fucking hug was going to break me down. So, like the caveman I was, I turned in her arms, took her face in my hands and kissed her.

The kiss was desperate and sad, and before long I pulled back. "I'm sorry," I said, feeling like I'd just used her.

She gave me a squinty smile. "Never apologize for kissing me."

"You know what I mean. I had this whole romantic weekend planned, and now this..." I shook my head. "We can stop talking about this now." I pulled away and wandered toward the table, opened the guest services booklet, but I felt her quietly watching me. "We can still go out..."

"We'll get to that in a minute," she said as she came up beside me. "Can I ask one more question?"

I glanced up and nodded.

"You never were curious when you became an adult, never thought to reach out to your mother?"

Part of me didn't like how interested she was in this topic, but I was the one who started it, so I answered honestly. "No. My dad told me enough stories about her that I just figured there was no point in it. She never wanted me to begin with."

Running a hand down my arms, she replied, "I might be overstepping here, but how do you know? If you've never really given her a chance to say her side of things..."

"Her side?" My tone was defensive. " She was an addict who put her child in danger because getting high meant more to her than taking care of me."

"You're right. I'm sorry," she said breathlessly. "It's just you must've loved her very much to go in that car after her.

You may have saved your mother's life that day. And it sounds like she tried to stop you from getting hurt."

Instinctively, I put a hand against my chest, feeling the raised bump through my shirt. "I don't know... It's just always been something that was easier to avoid than think about. She could've reached out to me as an adult, but she never did."

"Maybe she was ashamed. Maybe your dad threatened her to keep her away... Who knows?"

I narrowed my gaze at her, wondering why she was pushing me on this. "Look, I appreciate you listening, but I don't want to talk about this anymore. I only wanted you to understand why I reacted the way I did. It was a shock to see her. It all came flooding back." I slammed the book closed, then regretted it. "I'm sorry I ruined our evening."

Ava slipped her arms around my waist and gazed up at me. "Nothing's ever ruined when I'm with you. I just want to be with you, Alex."

Guilt suffused me. "Not like this... I had plans to—"

"Plans can be changed. We can order in..."

She was making this too easy, which made me feel worse. "We went from a romantic night, an exclusive restaurant, and now you're perfectly happy with sitting in a hotel room with me, eating an overcooked burger?"

"Yep."

I laughed. "That's why I love you," I blurted.

"I love you too," she said as if it were the most natural thing in the world.

"No, that's not what I mean." Emotion tightened my chest, and I took her face in my hands. "Dammit, Ava. Yes, I've loved you half my life, but this is different. I am *in love* with you! And I have been for as long as I can remember. I just never allowed myself to think about it. And when all these feelings came flooding out tonight... It was right there, front and center."

She smiled, widely this time, and her eyes glistened. "Do you know how long I've waited for you to say that?"

I pressed my lips to hers in a soft kiss. "About as long as I've been dying to say it. That's why I wanted tonight to be special, not some...reaction to an emotional situation."

She let out a sweet little chuckle. "Every time we've ever gotten close, it's been when emotions are high. Don't you know why that is?"

I shook my head, uncaring if I came off as the clueless male.

"Because, we're not just attracted to each other. We need each other. We're emotionally invested, and when one of us hurts, the other will do whatever we can to make that go away. So, if there ever was a time for us to be together for the first time, this is it."

"You really believe that?"

"I do. We waited a long time to be together, and if you

want to wait another day for you, I'm okay with that. But if you want to be with me, Alex, that's all I've ever wanted."

I pulled her close, buried my face in the crook of her neck and inhaled the fresh scent of her hair. "I don't know how I got so damn lucky…"

We held each other for long moments, the only sound our deep breathing. And when we finally pulled apart, she said, "Why don't we stay in, order room service…maybe watch a movie"—she grinned—"under a blanket…"

My mind shot back to that night on her couch, how she'd come apart from my touch alone, and I couldn't help but smile. "So, that's all you need, huh?"

"Um…no, that's just the appetizer this time."

Chapter Twenty-One

Ava

Looking in the mirror, I dabbed at my tears and then tried to salvage what makeup I had left. My heart was still reeling from the story Alex had told me only moments ago. Of course, my whole family knew bits and pieces of his early childhood history, and we all knew how controlling his father was despite the fact that he was also an absent parent. Thinking of my own parents gave me a wave of guilt. Why were Sammy and I so lucky and blessed to have the most wonderful parents, and Alex had two that probably never should have had a child? It wasn't the same, but my parents loved Alex like a son, and I was going to make sure I reminded him of that.

As I brushed my teeth and stared at myself in the mirror, a

burst of anger settled in my stomach as I thought of the times I had talked to Maggie, and she'd conveniently left that story out. My heart raced at her deception, and I wondered if or when I'd reach out and confront her about it. I supposed she didn't owe me anything, and her goal was merely to learn more about her son, but I still felt a bit... I wasn't sure. Maybe she'd had hopes for a reunion and didn't want me to discourage it.

I shook my head at myself. *You've meddled enough, haven't you?* At some point I would have to tell Alex everything that went down with his mom... But not tonight. Not after he'd just seen her, not after she had gotten him so upset, not after he just poured his heart out to me, and certainly not before the first time we made love together.

I sighed and turned from the mirror, unable to look at myself any longer. Who was I kidding? I knew there was a good chance that Alex would hate me, wouldn't want me anymore after he found out I'd gone behind his back and never told him. And I didn't want to risk at least having this one special night with him. Maybe it was selfish, or maybe I could look at it as me being there for him in any way I could, and telling him wouldn't accomplish that.

My mind made up, I slipped off my dress and out of my heels, planning to change into something more comfortable since we were going to eat and watch a movie, something I insisted on to give us both time to clear our minds. But when I saw the dress shirt Alex had worn on the trip here hanging on the back of the door, I couldn't resist.

I opened the bathroom door and stepped into the room, waiting for him to turn around. He was seated on the couch, watching some sports news on the TV. I grinned, thoughts of us sharing a space together sometime in the future flashing through my mind.

When he didn't turn, I cleared my throat.

He did a double take when he saw me, then stood. "Are you fucking kidding me right now?" He blew out a breath. "You're really going to make this hard on me, aren't you?"

I moved toward him slowly. "I thought I was doing the opposite."

When we reached each other, his arms went around my waist, mine around his neck. "Damn, my shirt never looked so good."

"Glad you don't mind. I like it because it smells like you."

He grinned and then dipped his head to capture my lips. His strong hands were splayed on my back, pressing me into his firm body. I'd longed for this moment for so many years my heart raced at the thought of Alex finally making me his. It was actually kind of surreal, so when Alex pulled back, it felt like he'd read my mind.

"I..." An awkward smile played on his lips.

"What?" I could feel his chest rise and fall between us.

He took my face in his hands. "This... Us. It's—"

"Hard to believe?"

He nodded. "Ava, I've watched you go from a girl to a woman to...the most amazing and beautiful person I've ever met. I just needed a beat, you know? I...want to do right by you."

My heart filled with warmth. "I know. But if you're worried if I'm sure...I've never wanted anything more in my life." Saying those words while his eyes were locked on mine was like a double shot of whiskey flying through my veins.

Alex's gaze narrowed for a second before he said, "Goddamn, Ava, if you knew how much I want you right now." He drew me back against him, then lifted me up. I gasped in delight and wrapped my legs around his waist as he walked us back over to the bed. We kissed for long moments before I felt him lower me to the ground. His eyes panned down to the top button of his shirt I wore, and he grinned. He undid the first button, then the second, his lips blazing a trail over my skin with each button lower, and when he finally pulled it away from my breast and lowered his mouth to me, my breath caught.

I held the back of his head to me, but he didn't linger long, instead kissing a trail down to my stomach until he was on his knees in front of me. He placed soft kisses on my stomach, and when he pressed his cheek against me and held me tightly, I felt my throat tighten with emotion.

I'd almost got lost in the moment, when I felt his fingers slide along the border of my panties and then slowly lower them to the floor, where I stepped out of them. When he raised back up to his full height, the hunger in his eyes set my whole body ablaze. Deftly, I unbuttoned his shirt, and when I pulled it away from his taut chest, my eyes homed in on the scar there. I ran my finger over the rigid surface, then placed a soft kiss on it. Alex's fingers weaved through my hair before he tilted my face up to his. He kissed me deeply, slowly, then as if a switch was flipped, he devoured me, and I moaned into his mouth. When his hands left my face, I heard him undoing his belt and then his pants.

Alex lowered me to the bed, settled on top of me, and stared into my eyes. One of his hands sought mine, and he laced our fingers together just before he connected our bodies and finally made us one. Everything about his movements felt so right, so good—the way we fit together so perfectly, the way our bodies instinctively found a seamless rhythm. And when he brought me to the height of pleasure, I didn't hold back, took everything he gave me, calling out his name as his head fell to the crook of my neck, and he joined me in an exquisite free fall.

After, as our bodies rested, still entwined in each other, I couldn't help but smile, even as a tear slid from the corner of my eye. As if he knew, he pulled me tighter against his body, and I couldn't imagine another moment more perfect than this.

Chapter Twenty-Two

Ava

Wearing the hotel robe, my hair still damp from the shower, I stood in the doorway of the bathroom, watching Alex sleep. Lying on his back, bare-chested with the sheet tucked at his waist, he looked like one of those dreamy magazine ads for cologne or...sheets.

When his eyes opened and quickly found mine, it seemed as though it were their sole purpose. I felt myself blush. Alex reached his hand out to me, and I stepped forward.

"You showered without me," he said when I took his hand. Then he yanked me to the bed so I landed halfway on top of him. My mouth went right to his, and we shared a deep kiss that took my breath away.

Alex pulled back, and I said, "I'm sorry. I don't want to be late to the office. We slept late…" Since I'd told my parents I was meeting with my boss, I figured I might as well while I was in Vegas.

He winced. "Damn, I'm sorry I forgot." He gave me a peck on the lips before sitting up. "I better get in there before I won't let either of us leave this bed."

I was tempted to blow off my appointment with my boss, even for just a few minutes in bed with Alex, especially with the replay of last night flashing in my mind. But he was already up, helping me be responsible.

"I'll be quick," he said before closing the door.

I realized too late that my makeup was in there. Were we at the stage of sharing bathroom space? I decided to pack instead. I knew he took fast showers anyway.

When I went to the side of the bed to grab my shoes, Alex's phone chimed on the nightstand. He had it set where a preview of texts showed on the screen. *I shouldn't look. Dammit, don't look, Ava.* I saw *Jessica*, and couldn't stop myself. I spun the phone so it wasn't upside down and read, *Honey, are you all right? Not like you to skip out on a Monday. Called your office…*

That was the bitch making herself comfortable in Alex's kitchen.

"Read anything interesting?"

I straightened and whirled around to him, my face burning hot. "I"—I shook my head—"have no excuse. I'm sorry."

"You don't trust me?" He tilted his head condescendingly but didn't look the least bit angry. In fact, he seemed pleased, which was probably worse for me and my embarrassment.

"No...I do. It's just. It was that Jessica woman."

"Oh..." I could have sworn I saw him hide a smirk. In gray sweatpants, his chest and hair still damp, he flew across the room, grabbed the phone, and flopped onto the bed. "Let's just do this thing, huh?" He patted the space next to him.

"Do what?" I climbed onto the bed next to him.

Alex pulled up his contacts list and then handed me the phone. "Go ahead. Look all you want. Ask me anything. I am an open book." He leaned over and pointed to my name, grinning. "See, you're right on top."

"That's because my name starts with *A*." I scrolled up a little. "But what about this Allison?"

He reached over and deleted her. "Gone."

I laughed and then scrolled more. "Do I even want to know what the ratio of business to pleasure is?"

"Honestly, it doesn't matter." He put one arm behind his head, and his muscle bulged deliciously. "This is going to make me sound like an ass, but most of the women in that phone were just me killing time."

"Come on..." I elbowed him lightly.

"I'm serious. You don't have to believe me, but a lot of times I was just distracting myself, waiting for the universe to deliver you to my doorstep. And that's exactly what happened."

I turned to him, mouth agape, and then pinched his side. "Oh my gosh. So if I didn't come home, you never would've come after me?"

He shrugged a shoulder. "I didn't think I was good enough for you, Ava. I didn't want to hurt you, and I knew your parents wouldn't want us together."

Still holding the phone, I turned on my side to face him. "You don't know that. They love you, and besides they didn't like Mark at first either. And then they ended up loving him."

Alex turned then. "That's because Sammy and I told your parents that he cheated on his taxes, and that instead of adopting a puppy, he bought one from a puppy mill for three grand."

When he smiled proudly, I pushed against his chest. "Oh, my God. You did not."

"Ask your brother."

Flabbergasted, I turned my attention back to the

phone, setting it on the bed between us. I scrolled to a few other women's names: Bri, Cat, Erica. He deleted two of the three. Then I scrolled until I got to Jessica and then stared at Alex pointedly.

"I honestly don't know what her deal is. She flirts with everyone, and she's the kind of person to use sex to get what she wants. I'm sorry I still have to put up with her until I close the deal with her dad. I could delete her, but it won't matter."

I pursed my mouth. "Fine." I scrolled more and stopped when I saw Lauren. "That's the girl from the bar. She's beautiful."

"Not as beautiful as you." He leaned in and brushed a kiss over my neck.

"Are you going to delete her?" Not that I expected him to, but when he was so freely offering...

"Honestly, I don't want to." His gaze held mine. "She's a good person, and she's cool to be around, and I'd like to have her as a friend."

"You went on a date with her, and she kissed you right in front of me."

"Yeah, but she didn't know we were together, and she went in there to explain it to you... We went on one date, and I talked about you the whole time."

I couldn't help but smile. "That's what she said." She

did seem like a genuine person. I was just about to tell him I didn't expect him to rid all women from his life when he started laughing. "What?"

"You don't get to be jealous of my female friends."

"Why not?" I asked merely out of curiosity.

"Because you have Gunnar, and I'm just supposed to be cool with that. So, I get to keep Lauren." He smiled proudly like we were trading players in some fantasy football league.

Yes, it irked me that he was right, and I was a little jealous, but I didn't have a leg to stand on. "Can't argue with that." I handed his phone back.

"But we only got to L."

"We don't have time and besides, I trust you." Of course I didn't say I was worried I'd have to pull up my contacts, and I couldn't remember if I'd saved one for his mom, Maggie. "And I'm sorry you have to wait around for me while I'm in my office, but it shouldn't take long."

"It's all right," he said, getting up. "I've got some calls I can make anyway." Alex caught me in his arms when I got off the bed. "I just wish we had more time in this room." Sliding his hand over my ass, he pressed me into him.

I allowed myself a moment to feel his strong shoulders, breathe in his fresh scent, but then his mouth was on mine, and I gave in to him. His kiss was hungry, but he didn't move to take it further, probably because he knew we were pressed for time. When one of his hands teased along my hip, I couldn't deny either of us any longer. I pulled back and gazed up at him as I released the tie on my robe.

Alex slipped it off my shoulders and gaped at my naked body in front of him. "Damn, baby…"

Chapter Twenty-Three

Alex

"Listen, I'm sorry to cut this short," I told the private investigator, "but someone just walked into my office. Do what you can for now and let me know what you find out." I ended the call and had just set the phone down on my desk when Dax came running toward me and took a flying leap into my lap.

It wasn't unusual for Sammy to stop by my office unannounced, but I didn't want to explain why I had been on the phone with a PI. After seeing my mother and telling Ava everything, I decided to do a little digging and see what I could find out about her. But that didn't mean I was ready to share my story with everyone in the family.

Still, a twinge of guilt sat in my gut about keeping this

—not to mention that I was seeing his sister—from my best friend. There'd never been anybody in my life that I was as close to as I was Sammy. But now that he had family and so many responsibilities, we had drifted apart some, which was why I never minded these surprise visits.

I stood up with Dax in my arms and walked him over to the top shelf of my bookcase. He knew when he came here that he got to have a mini bag of peanut M&Ms because we had a gentleman's agreement that he would behave in my office. It definitely was not a bribe.

Once he snagged one from the jar, I set him down, and he ran over to the small table. He climbed up into the chair as I closed the distance between Sammy and me. We gave each other a quick hug and slap on the back, and when we pulled apart and exchanged a grin, I said, "Hey, man. Good to see you."

"Yeah, seems like we've both been too busy to check in, and since Dax and I were on our own today, I thought I'd stop by."

I knew the guy well enough to be able to tell when he wasn't putting it all out there, so I narrowed my eyes at him. "Glad you did, but are you sure that's all there is?" My pulse spiked the second I finished speaking. Why the hell would I prompt him to talk when there were things I couldn't talk about? I was asking for trouble.

"Actually, I ran into someone at Dax's preschool today."

"Oh yeah?" I showed him a dubious expression. I sensed where this was going. Sammy and Cass were forever trying to find me a wife, so we could all have dinners at each other's houses and go on storybook vacas together.

He glanced at the table to check on his son. "Guess who just started teaching at the preschool?"

I was already behind the eight ball from missing a day of work, so I didn't really have time for games. "Why don't you just tell me." I sat on the edge of the table and stole a yellow M&M from Dax. My little buddy never got mad about it—he actually liked it, and he let out an adorable giggle.

Sammy went to reach for a red one, and Dax scooted his pile away.

I laughed and then gave Dax a fist bump.

Shaking his head, Sammy said, "Do you remember Denise Moreno?"

I grinned at the memories that name drew from me. "No way. Denise is back in town? I thought she moved away?"

"Yeah, she's been back a few months now." He flashed a huge smile. "We only talked for a few minutes, but she asked about you."

Denise and I had never dated, but she was sweet and hot, and we both knew I'd been attracted to her. Only reason I never asked her out was because she'd always been with someone. What was I supposed to say that wouldn't make Sammy suspicious? "And..."

"And...this is your chance to ask her out." He pulled his phone from his back pocket and my pulse quickened.

I stood abruptly. "Bro, you didn't tell her I'd call, did you?"

He glanced up from the phone, brows raised. "I mean no, but..." He shrugged. "She gave me her number, so..."

"She's expecting me to reach out." My tone was defensive, but I couldn't help it.

"What's the big deal?" He tilted his head and stared at me silently for a few beats, then said, "So, you are seeing someone. What the hell, who is she?"

I shook my head and grabbed another M&M to stall.

"Daddy said 'hell,'" Dax said to me, his face strained and confused.

"I know. I heard him."

Sammy sat down next to his son. "Why do you hear everything except what Mommy and Daddy want you to?"

"Huh?" He tilted his head. "Can I play?" He pointed to Sammy's phone.

Sighing, Sammy pulled up a game and set it in front of

Dax, but I knew the sidetrack wouldn't stick. Thankfully, my office phone rang at that moment, and I went to my desk and took the call. It didn't take long, and when I ended the call, I said, "I've got a meeting in about ten minutes." I inwardly cringed because it sounded like I was trying to get rid of them.

Sammy stayed at the table, and I remained leaning against the front of my desk, the weight of my deception heavy on my shoulders. I could tell Sammy everything right now, but would Ava be upset I didn't give her a heads up? Before I could say anything, Sammy clapped his hands.

"Oh... It's that blonde. The one from the bar, right? What's her name?"

It took me a moment to catch up to his line of thinking, and then it hit me. "Lauren."

"Right. So, it must be pretty serious if you're turning down a shot at Denise." He grinned.

I was stunned, though it made sense he'd come to that conclusion. But this took us into a whole new category of deception. If I let him believe Lauren and I were involved, then it was lying versus just an omission. I racked my brain for what to say. "Sammy..." I sighed.

"Whoa, what's wrong with your face?" He laughed. "Never seen you so jacked up over a woman."

"What's jack up?" Dax said, looking up from his game.

Sammy laughed and patted Dax on the head. "It's sort of like when you're confused and not feeling like yourself." Then he quickly added, "But it's not a good thing for a little boy to say...so don't." Sammy stood then and came over to me. "When you figure it all out, let me know, yeah?" His gaze held mine, like he knew this was complicated, and I appreciated that. Sammy was always the wiser of the two of us.

"Thanks, man." I slapped my hand on his shoulder and gripped it tightly. "I know we haven't been hanging as much the last few years..." Words were hard, and that was probably the best I could pull off in that moment.

"It's all good. You're my brother, always will be. No matter what." He nodded, and it felt both comforting and unsettling, if that were possible. "Hope you know that," he added.

"I do. And I feel the same."

"Well, we'll get out of your hair." He moved back to the table and started to corral a reluctant Dax.

As I hugged Dax at the door, Sammy said, "Hope to see you at my parents' for dinner next Saturday." I told him I'd be there, and as they were walking out the door, he said, "And bring your woman, if you want..."

Shit.

For a second I did a mental double-take. Had he purposely said "woman" instead of Lauren?

Chapter Twenty-Four

Alex

I knocked quietly at the door in case anyone was sleeping. It wasn't that late but late enough, especially for an unexpected visitor. I hadn't even planned to show up at Ava's place, and I hadn't given her a heads up either, partly because I'd been in the car and partly because...I guess I just wanted to surprise her.

I had been working late, going over the final details of one of my deals, and for some reason, I found myself heading here instead of home. Now that Ava and I were together, the quiet of my place just wasn't appealing. Plus, I hated being away from her. Like it physically hurt.

After a minute, the door popped open, but it wasn't Ava standing there. Gunnar wore a pair of gym shorts and no shirt. *Of course.* Is this how he walked around the place all the time?

I tried not to react and instead said, "Hey, man, can I come in?"

He opened the door wider and said, "Mi casa es su casa."

"Thanks." I didn't doubt he was staring at my ass as I entered, and when I turned around and saw the look on his face, it solidified my assumption.

I'd seen Ava's car in the parking lot, but I still said, "Is she here?"

"Who? Madonna?" He gave me a half grin before adding, "Yeah, but it's pretty quiet, so she may have fallen asleep. She was reading in bed."

Since I was supposed to be trying to get along with the guy, I asked, "What are you watching?" I gestured to the TV, which was paused.

He stretched and ran a hand down his taut stomach. "You wouldn't believe me if I told you."

"Try me."

"I'm watching the first *Hangover*."

"What? I love those movies," I told him, honestly.

"Ava does too," he said, walking around the back of the couch, then collapsing into a corner. "Bet you didn't know that."

I wasn't sure why he was suddenly turning

confrontational when I was trying to be cool, so I just shrugged. But he wasn't even looking at me, too busy picking up the remote.

"They're pretty stupid, but I love the group of guys and how different they all are but also great friends. Plus, you gotta love them being in Vegas, right?"

"Oh, yeah that's right." I waited until he glanced up and then said, "Mind if I head back," ticking my head toward the hallway.

This time he shrugged, so I took the opportunity to escape and headed down the hall to Ava's room.

Opening the door slowly revealed long sleek legs only covered by some short pajama bottoms. The room was dimly lit, aglow with candles burning on her nightstand. I would have to talk to her about how dangerous that was, since clearly she'd fallen asleep.

Ava was lying on her side in the middle of the bed, which seemed like fate left me a space right behind her. I slipped my shoes off and eased onto the bed, spooning right up next to her. I assumed that would wake her and when it didn't, I took the opportunity to gaze down at her as I propped myself up on an elbow.

I brushed a gentle finger across her forehead to move her hair back from her face. Damn, she was so fucking beautiful it took my breath away.

Unable to help myself, I smoothed my hand down her hip and softly caressed her thigh as I bent and pressed my lips to her neck. I honestly couldn't believe she wasn't waking up.

At some point, I'd just purposely wake her, especially since I was already getting myself worked up.

Keeping my mouth near her neck, I lightly brushed my tongue behind her ear. Instinctively, I gripped her hip tighter and pressed up closer so her ass was snug against me. "Ava," I whispered and then peppered slow kisses down her neck.

This wasn't what I'd planned on the way over here, but damn... I felt my breathing grow heavy, the blood thrum through my veins, and I knew I better get this girl awake and fast.

I ran my hand up her hip and around to her stomach, slipping beneath her loose tank. "Baby," I whispered into her ear.

She stirred then and turned her head just enough for her parted lips to find mine, and I took her mouth in a long deep kiss.

It was me who pulled back first—because I needed to see her face—and when she blinked up at me with that angelic face of hers, it was worth the wait.

"Hey, baby..." I ran my thumb across her bottom lip.

She smiled. "I like hearing you call me that." Turning her body to face me, she ran her hand up my chest, then leaned in and kissed my neck. "This is a nice surprise. I thought I was dreaming at first, but this is even better." She started unbuttoning my shirt.

I chuckled. "I swear I didn't just come here for a booty call."

This time she laughed. "That's something else I never thought I'd hear you say." Pulling back, she added, "So, why did you come?"

"I missed you. I can't stay away from you, Ava. And..." I reached into my pocket and pulled out a small rectangular box. "I wanted to bring you this."

Her brows knitted as she sat up. "What? What did you do?"

"Just open it."

As if she'd instantly flipped from confused to excited, she snatched the box and opened it. Staring down at the Venetian link platinum bracelet, she said, "Oh, my God, Alex..." Then she turned to me, her eyes glazed over. "But... How did you..." She lifted it gently from the box.

I sat up and leaned my back against the wall. "I saw you staring at it when we were in Vegas. And I heard you say something to the salesperson about how much you love it. It's not a big deal. I...just wanted you to have it."

"It's stunning." She held it up to me, then frowned.

"And it's too much. Alex, you shouldn't be spending this much money on me."

"That's what money's for," I said. "What else am I going to spend it on?" Truthfully, when I saw that look on her face, I knew I had to get it. It was terrifying to know you'd do anything to make someone you love happy, but there was nothing I could do. I was done for. Ava was everything. She always had been, always would be. But I shrugged and said, "Think of it as making up for all those lame birthday presents I gave you in the past."

She coughed out a laugh. "Oh, like when you gave me long johns for my eighteenth birthday?"

I couldn't help but laugh. "You needed some coverage." I supposed on some level I was trying to keep my little gem under wraps from all the other insatiable assholes out there.

Her grin grew wider, and she rose up on her knees. "Will you put it on me?" Then she threw a leg over my lap and straddled my thighs so she was facing me.

I took it from her, hopelessly ignoring the fire she set when she crawled on top of me.

Once I had it on her, she said, "It's stunning."

I swept a hand through her hair to hook behind her neck, then pulled her mouth to mine, saying against her lips, "You're the stunning one."

We shared a few soft kisses, Ava's hands gripping my

biceps, mine bracing against her back. When she moaned into my mouth, I broke the kiss, and we exchanged a knowing grin.

"Thank you, Alex. I should have said that sooner."

"You're welcome."

"Now, I think I was in the middle of unbuttoning your shirt," she said with a half grin.

"You first," I shot back. Then I lifted her tank over her head, revealing her naked full breasts. Not giving her a chance to reach for my buttons I leaned forward, connecting my mouth with a piece of heaven. As much as I wanted to linger there, I was growing impatient, and by the sounds of Ava's moans and heavy breathing she was too. "Let's get you out of these," I said, sliding her shorts over her hips.

She lifted to help me and let out a giggle when we struggled to get them off, but then she was quickly back in place, undoing my belt and pants, as if she were racing against the clock.

Leaning over me, her hair dangling on each side of my face, she brought her mouth to mine, and we kissed as I slowly guided her onto me.

"God, I love being inside you," I whispered.

She held my gaze as she moved atop me, and our slow rhythmic start morphed into a frantic crescendo sending us both flying. And when I brought her down to hold against my chest, I thought it would explode with all the emotions I was feeling. I'd always thought I loved Ava, but this... This was unexplainable with words. Still, as I stroked her bare back, and we regained our breathing, I told her, "I love you, Ava."

Chapter Twenty-Five

Ava

Cass came out of the back, holding a tray full of double chocolate chip muffins and refilled the case to my right.

"How are you doing, girl?" she asked me with a smile. Only Cass could be genuinely happy, even though she'd been baking since three in the morning.

I gave the customer their boxed order and told her, "I'm good." Then, I glanced over to Gunnar, who was sitting at one of the tables, eating a chocolate-filled croissant next to Dax. "How about you, Gunnar? Are you hanging in there?" I asked sarcastically.

We had both arrived around six to help with the

fundraiser the bakery was having for the pediatric unit at the hospital my mom worked at.

With his mouth full, Gunnar nodded, finished chewing, and then swallowed. Gesturing to his stomach, he said, "You've seen these abs...all this muscle needs fuel. And if I don't get sustenance after exerting myself, I shut down." He handed a napkin to Dax. "Plus, I'm keeping the little guy company, right?"

Dax popped a donut hole into his mouth and nodded with a big grin that rivaled his mother's. He was enjoying Gunnar's company entirely too much, and I could already see that would be another reason for Alex to feel threatened by him.

Cass laughed. "Well, we appreciate any help at all." She carried her empty tray to the back.

Sammy had just finished wiping down some tables and was coming around the counter to help me fill orders and run the cash register, when I saw Alex walk through the door.

We exchanged a secretive grin, and a little thrill of excitement shot through me. The giddy feeling was new to me, something I hadn't experienced with other men I'd dated, not even Mark.

I tried not to stare at him, but the man had always drawn eyes from women wherever he went. I just hoped Sammy didn't notice my behavior. Alex and I hadn't really been around the family that much since we'd been together, and I wasn't sure how we would be able to pull it off without drawing suspicion. We also hadn't worried about having the hard conversations yet—even though it was starting to feel like it was time—and just wanted to enjoy every moment together we had before all the complications started.

When I took another peek, I saw that Alex had gotten in line behind three people. We made eyes at each other as I helped an older gentleman who couldn't make up his mind. Sammy was busy chatting and ringing up customers, so he didn't notice, I was sure.

Thankfully, by the time Alex got to the front, Gunnar had jumped up and came behind the counter. It was a bit crowded for three people, so I moved to the very end of the display case to talk with Alex.

I often saw him in a suit but typically without the jacket that he wore now, and damn his shoulders were heavenly. The suit, midnight blue with a crisp white shirt and silver-blue tie, looked like it was tailor-made for him. I almost had to shake my head to remove the image of me undressing him. His half-grin felt like he was reading my mind, the cocky bastard.

"What are you doing here?" I lifted my brows.

"I'm gonna get a dozen," Alex said, gesturing to the

donuts. "Plus, I heard there was some hot little thing working behind the counter."

Heat rushed to my cheeks. He'd said it quietly enough, but I still shot my gaze over to Sammy to see if he had heard.

"Uh...that's kind of you—for the fundraiser, I mean." Yeah, I sounded formal and awkward, and I hated it. All I wanted to do was hug him and before "us," I probably would have and now I felt like I couldn't.

"Okay...I promised your mom, and I figured I might as well bring some donuts for my team. I've been riding their asses a little hard lately with this deal."

"Oh, yeah, when is that going to be done?" I knew finishing that deal wouldn't guarantee he never had to deal with Jessica again, but I blurted it out anyway.

"Three weeks maybe," he said with a grin.

As Alex slowly and meticulously picked out each of his dozen donuts, our eyes kept catching each other's and holding little conversations.

When he was done, he added, "Four of those Apple Fritters, too, please."

I'd needed two boxes to fit everything, and once I had it packaged up, I moved to the cash register, set them in front of Sammy, then pretended to clean the area around the coffee maker while Sammy rang up Alex, and Gunnar helped someone else.

"Hey, man," Sammy said to Alex.

"Great turnout." He handed Sammy his card. "Are we still on for the cigar room on Friday?"

I was surprised because I didn't know anything about that—not that he had to run his plans by me.

"About that..." Sammy said.

As Sammy ran the card, Alex said, "You're not backing out on me, are you?"

"Not backing out, but what if we hit the cigar room next time and do a double date, me and Cass and you and Lauren?"

My mouth flew open, but thankfully, Sammy couldn't see me behind him. Gunnar must have been listening, too, because he shot me a look. I tried not to let it affect me, but why the hell would Sammy think Lauren and Alex were dating? Then my brain shot back to that kiss at the bar. Alex must not have set him straight, and I knew why. It wasn't a big deal... Unless they actually went on a date, and that was where I would draw the damn line with this charade.

My pulse raced as I waited for Alex's answer; the adrenaline almost had me speaking up, claiming my man right there in front of Sammy and all these strangers.

"I think I can handle my own dating life."

"Can you?" Gunnar said, and we all snapped our heads to him. He winced and said, "Oops," then handed a woman her coffee and pretended everything was perfectly normal.

Alex picked up his boxes from the counter. "Thanks, man, but let's stick with the cigar room. Should be fun and we can...catch up." Alex's eyes darted to me, and I hoped that meant he was thinking the same thing I was. The longer we kept us a secret the worse it would be when everyone found out.

"Yeah, sure," Sammy said. "Talk soon..."

There was a woman behind Alex itching to order so that took Sammy's attention as Alex moved away from the counter. I didn't want him to go yet, but I knew he had to. Moving to the side counter, I watched him stop at the table where Dax was seated. He set his boxes down, gave Dax a hug, and the two exchanged words I couldn't hear.

The rush had died down, but when the door opened, I took my gaze over that way on instinct. Then I almost gasped, my jaw slacking for the second time that morning.

It was Mark.

Chapter Twenty-Six

Alex

I had to do a double-take when I saw Mark enter the bakery. *What the hell is he doing here?* My chest tightened as the obvious answer punched me right in the gut. Of course, he'd show up at some point. Any man in their right mind wouldn't let a woman like Ava go without a fight.

I took my gaze over to my woman. *That's right, asshole, she's mine now.* I didn't have anything against the guy, really, so my anger didn't make sense. Ava looked just as shocked as I was. Instead of getting in line, Mark moved to the far side of the bakery, where a decorative shelf lined the wall and housed framed pictures, bakery utensils, and some prepackaged goods.

My pulse was pounding, and I couldn't help but wonder if it was more fear than anger, that somehow he'd convince Ava to give him another chance. After all, it sounded like Mark hadn't done anything wrong—other than not being me, obviously—and he'd wanted to marry her.

I eyed the door as Ava made her way over to Mark to greet him, knowing I should go before Sammy or Cass saw how worked up I was getting. Then, I made a split-second decision when Mark gestured toward the door. I said a quick goodbye to Dax, grabbed my boxes—conveniently leaving my keys on the table next to him—then quickly headed out of the bakery ahead of them.

My car was on the street but close enough I could see the front of the bakery. I set my boxes on the hood of the car and just as I turned, Ava and Mark walked out and then moved off to the side of the door.

Ava didn't notice me watching at first, and although I couldn't hear everything they were saying, Ava's body language was clear enough: she was uncomfortable. Which meant I wasn't going anywhere. I pretended to check my pockets for my keys, even though I knew I'd left them on the table in the bakery.

Fuck it. I couldn't wait any longer. Leaving the boxes of donuts on the hood of my car, I strode back to the bakery. Ava's gaze caught mine over Mark's shoulder and widened. I honestly wasn't sure what I was going to do, only that I needed to do something, not to mention this was a wakeup call that it was time to make Ava and me official and pray the family accepted it, accepted me.

Ava opened her mouth and drew in air just as I arrived at Mark's back. But nothing came out, and then Mark turned.

"Alex?" Mark said, narrowing his gaze on me.

"Mark..." I held his stare for longer than was socially acceptable, then said, "Forgot my keys inside." I gestured with my head to the door. And yet, even though I'd announced it, I just stood there, staring at Mark. "So, what are you doing here?" I darted my eyes to Ava, knowing she'd hate that I'd asked, and sure enough her face was pinched, her mouth forming wrinkles.

Instead of answering me, Mark pivoted and stepped next to Ava. "We were sort of in the middle of something, if you don't mind." He showed one of those closed-mouth half grins. "Plus you don't want someone to get ahold of those keys and take off in your Mercedes."

"Yeah," Ava said, her voice a little shaky. "And tell Sammy, I'll be back in a minute..." Her eyes seemed to plead with me to leave.

Standing in place for a few more awkward beats, I contemplated telling Mark to get lost before I kicked him all the way back to Vegas. But it wasn't my place. At least I knew that was what Ava would think. I hated the idea of leaving them alone, of him pleading his case, but I just had to have faith it was all pointless. Ava had chosen me, and she would tell him that or some version of it. "No problem." I gave them a single nod and headed back inside.

Cass was with Dax when I returned, holding my keys. I couldn't quite read the look on her face, but when she handed them to me, she said, "Didn't work, huh?"

"What?" My pulse quickened like I'd been caught with my hand in the cookie jar. Could she know?

A sly grin took over her face. "Your car... Didn't work without the keys, right?"

Her brows lifted, and I got a strange feeling she was throwing double meanings at me. I took the keys from her hand. "Thanks." I gave Dax a fist bump, and just as I turned away, Cass's words caught me.

"Should I give her five minutes and then send Sammy out?"

I threw a grin over my shoulder. "Make it two."

Someone was coming in as I approached the door, and they held it open for me. I could see just beyond; Mark took Ava's hand. My blood pressure shot heat over my skin, but I felt powerless. Ava had always been annoyed with my knee-jerk reactions, my temper, and this could be a defining moment for us.

Walking out, I started to head to my car as I kept eyes on Ava. Of course, she had that sweet expression, that look of empathy that came from her caring heart, and I hoped he wouldn't get the wrong idea from it.

Okay, maybe I was an idiot, but I stopped and turned back. As I walked up, I heard him saying, "...it's all I ask...please."

"I don't know..." Ava said just before she saw me approach again.

"I'm only here for one night."

"Yeah, that's not going to work, Mark," I said a little too loudly.

Ava's eyes went wide, and Mark turned to me.

"Alex." Mark said my name like it was that vegetable on your plate you didn't want invading all your favorite foods. "Thought you were leaving."

"I am. But I was just going to tell Ava that Cass needs her inside."

He turned to her. "I'm sorry I'm keeping you. So, can you meet me for a drink so we can talk?"

My eyes bore into Ava's face; even though she was looking at him, I was sure she sensed me willing her to get rid of him once and for all. I knew Ava, though, and she was too nice to cut him off so abruptly.

So, it was a total shock when she said, "Mark, I'm sorry you came all the way here, but I don't have anything more to say. It's just not going to happen." Her eyes dropped to her wrist where she was fiddling with something and when I followed her gaze, I noticed it was the bracelet I'd given her.

Pride—and a large dose of relief—swelled inside me, and I fought to hide my grin.

Mark dropped his chin to his chest. "Don't apologize, Ava. I just had to try." He took a step back, then turned to me. "You don't deserve her."

I glanced at Ava, whose jaw slacked.

Before I could respond, he looked at Ava again. "And he'll never give you what I could have." Then he walked away.

We stared at each other a beat before I said, "Well, that wasn't what I expected."

She sighed. "Yeah, and if Mark figured it out, I wonder who else did."

Chapter Twenty-Seven

Ava

I snuck a peek at my phone, which rested on the counter, so Gunnar wouldn't see me. "Do you know if these dishes are clean or dirty?" I asked, pulling the door open.

"Neither," he said from his perch on a barstool. He dug into his microwaved lasagna and then took a big bite.

Looking inside at the empty racks, I said, "Oh."

"How late is he?"

I sighed and leaned my elbows on the counter. "Forty-five minutes."

"No text... No call?"

I shook my head. The average woman might have gotten worried if she hadn't heard from her boyfriend, who was supposed to pick her up for a date, but Alex often worked late into the night and sometimes got caught in meetings with clients. It wouldn't be the first time this happened, but I never cared before.

"So, what are you going to do?" He shoved the cardboard container toward me. "Wanna share my dinner?"

I managed a small grin for his kindness.

Alex and I were supposed to have the serious talk about how and when we'd tell the family about us. I wouldn't voice this to Gunnar, but in the back of my mind was a little voice that said Alex had changed his mind about us, that it was all too much for him to face my parents and Sammy. "Thank you. No." Sighing, I straightened and grabbed my phone. "How hard is it to send a text?" I'd sent him two and called once, and even that, I worried, was too much.

"Not that hard." He pointed his fork at me. "And I was just starting to like the guy too."

"What? You said you liked him." I tilted my head.

"Let's just say, he rides a fine line." He wiped his mouth with a napkin, then added, "Now the jury's out until I see how tonight plays out."

I wasn't the best with being patient, so I grabbed my keys, phone, and purse. "I can't just sit around here."

"You going to his office?"

"No, I'm going to his house." I had a key, and I would decide on the way over if I would use it or not.

He swiveled on the stool as I passed him. "Call me if you need backup."

"I will," I said over my shoulder and headed out the door.

At Alex's place, I sat in my car, trying to decide if I was the same Ava who knew exactly who Alex was and what his life was like... Or, was I Ava the girlfriend, who had expectations? The former would have me going inside, getting naked, and waiting for him on his couch with a bottle of wine. Obviously, that Ava was more fun, less complicated. And yet I didn't move. I'd settled once before—with Mark. Yes, this was different, and Alex had told me he wanted to make this work, but had he really understood what that meant?

My phone chimed, and I snatched it up. I'd texted Alex before I left that I was coming here, would wait thirty minutes, and then I was going home and to bed. That was twenty minutes ago.

Alex: *On my way...*

I stared at it, waiting to see if there would be more. "That's it?"

My irritation was growing by the minute. Even though I knew at least he was alive and on his way, still, I sat in my car. I was irritated, but I couldn't go home until I heard his excuse—*uh, reason.*

When Alex finally arrived, I opened my window as he approached my car.

"I'm sorry," he said instead of a greeting. "It couldn't be helped."

Narrowing my gaze, I felt my blood pressure spike. "Did Jessica have you gagged and bound to a chair?"

"Jessica?" He pulled his head back, ran a hand through his hair. "She wasn't even there." He sighed. "Could we not make this—"

"What? Into a thing? Well, from where I'm sitting...it *is* a thing."

"You didn't have to come here." His gaze darted around the lot.

"Yeah, I could have sat home, waiting by the phone like a good girl. Is that what the other girls did before me?"

Shaking his head, he pulled his lips into a tight line. "Can we go inside to talk...please?"

"Haven't decided if I'm staying." I faced forward and stared through the dark windshield.

He leaned over, rested his forearms on the opened window. "Ava..." He placed a soft kiss on my cheek as I continued to look forward. It would be so easy to let him charm his way out of this, but I was still annoyed. "Please... I said I was sorry. I was at work and—"

"Then why do you smell like cigars?"

"Come on, Ava. You know how some of these meetings are. We had both Carl and his brother in Derrick's office. It was impromptu, and I didn't have my phone. I couldn't think of any excuse to leave. Either they'd think another client was more important than they were, or they'd think it was personal, and their business wasn't as important."

I turned to him and tilted my head. "Some people think business *isn't* as important as personal. I guess you're not one of those people?"

He straightened and blew out a breath, staring up at the sky. "I've been working on this deal since before we were together. Are you saying I should just let it go down the toilet?"

It was my turn to sigh because I knew where he was going with that. But at the same time, I didn't want a life of being second to his career. "No, of course not. It's just that..." And then it hit me why this bothered me so much. "I don't even know what we are, like are we even a couple? Am I even allowed to be annoyed that this happened?" I held his gaze and waited.

A sexy half grin transformed his expression. "Are you saying you wanna be my girlfriend?"

I couldn't help but laugh. "Well, I sort of thought I already was."

With another quick glance over his shoulder, he kneeled down and held a hand out to me. "Ava Steadman…will you be my girlfriend?"

I felt a blush take my cheeks as I popped open the door, enough to get out but so I wouldn't hit him. "Will you get up before you ruin those pants?"

"That's not an answer," he said, gazing up at me.

I threw a hand on my hip. "So, you're saying you want to make this official…as in tell people?"

"That's exactly what I'm saying." His tone was serious, and he must have read the concern in my eyes because he added, "And, yes, I'm still worried about the family, but I believe in us, and I'll convince them we're the real deal."

I took his hand and pulled. "We'll convince them."

"Hell, yeah, we will!"

Alex's voice carried in the night, and I flinched. "Shh!"

"Hell, no. I just claimed my woman." Then he gave me a celebratory slap on the ass.

"Oww!"

Pulling on my arm, he hiked me over his shoulder and called, "And now I'm taking her back to my cave."

"Alex!" I screamed and tried to gasp his shoulders, afraid of falling.

And then he slapped my ass again and took off toward his apartment.

Chapter Twenty-Eight

Alex

Ava spread the blanket down over the sand, and then I dropped the backpack on top of it. I had carried both of those things as well as two chairs and a towel, while Ava only carried her sandals. She'd told me it was my penance for being late tonight, and I had accepted it with a grin because I would've done it anyway. My girl wasn't going to lift a finger in my presence.

I watched as she sat on her knees and dug things out of the backpack—which I'd mostly prepared in the morning before work—waiting until she got to the surprise I knew would please her, especially after our argument. I would have hated that to go to waste.

She didn't disappoint when she squealed and pulled

out the container. "Please tell me these are chocolate budino tarts."

I nodded, confirming I'd brought one of her all-time favorite desserts.

"But they're so hard to find." She opened the top and took a big sniff. "Mmm." Her grin grew wider, and she reached her hand out to me. "I can't believe you did all this." She laughed. "And it could've all gone to waste."

I sat down next to her, ran a hand up her back. "Yeah, you almost blew it."

Her mouth flew open, and I laughed. "You know I'm kidding. I might be a screw-up sometimes, but I know what my girl wants...and needs."

Ava set the carton down and took my face into her hands before placing a soft kiss on my lips. "Thank you," she whispered, lingering there, "but don't talk about yourself like that..."

This woman... The breeze kicked up and mercifully cooled my heated skin. We'd been there five minutes, and I was already itching to get her naked. I nuzzled her neck and drew in her scent.

She was more concerned about the dessert at the moment and turned back to the backpack, adding, "Only I am allowed to put you down like that."

"Fair enough." I pulled out a digital candle, turned it on, and set it on the blanket.

We shared the chocolate tarts along with a perfectly paired beer, which we drank from the bottle. I always did love watching her chug a beer. I wasn't worried about driving home because I planned to make the most of this beautiful night with my gorgeous girlfriend. We were in a pretty secluded spot, especially for this time of night and this late in the fall.

We had easy conversation, almost as if neither of us wanted to broach the subject we were supposed to be discussing. It just felt so right to finally be together and feel like we were a real couple, but this thing wouldn't go away.

Ava must have noticed my inner debate because she said, "Are you sure you're up for doing this? Telling the family, I mean."

I took her hand. "I won't lie. I'm a little worried...for all the reasons I've already said. But, hey, we already passed the first relationship test, so that should count for something, right?"

She tilted her head. "Test?"

"Yeah, we had our first fight and survived."

"You survived," she said, pushing against my chest.

Locking a hand around her wrist, I yanked her body against mine. "You're a tough adversary, Ava, but I haven't revealed all my power yet."

She gazed into my eyes, her chest drawing in a deep breath. "Well, I can't wait for that."

The heady tone of her voice satisfied me, and I closed my mouth over hers. She responded instantly, letting out a little moan as I held her, and we kissed. She was wedged between my legs, wriggling in all the right spots as our kiss grew hungry, frantic. When she pulled away, our eyes met and held for several seconds. I knew in that moment, I could spend the rest of my life looking into the depths of those gorgeous eyes. "I wish I had words to fully explain what I feel for you, Ava." I could hear how breathless my words were, but I didn't care.

"I think I know," she said quietly. "I just hope..."

I knew what she was thinking. It was the only dark cloud in this whole thing, but I didn't want her to worry or feel responsible. "There's nothing we can do but be honest." I brushed a lock of hair from her face. "I love Sue and Denny and Sammy...you... You're my family. My only family. But, there isn't anything I'd give up to be with you. I'd risk the world for you, Ava." A tear slid down her cheek, and I brushed it away with my thumb.

"You shouldn't have to," she said, a hint of desperation in her tone. "I'm banking on all of us. My parents love you like a son, and if we don't make it—"

I crushed my mouth to hers, kissed her long and hard before easing her down onto her back. "Don't you dare say it." I peered down at the most incredible woman I'd ever known. "We're making it, damn it." I shook my head when her mouth parted to speak. "That's final, Ava." Then I placed kiss after kiss on her mouth, her neck, her collar bone as I worked to relieve her of her clothes. She was stunning under the moonlight, and my heart almost couldn't take it.

We made love under the cloudless sky with the sounds of crashing waves muffling her cries as we reached that pinnacle together, holding each other as close as two people could.

After, we lay on the blanket, me on my back, Ava with her head resting on my chest. *If this is the only moment I ever have with Ava, I'll be the luckiest man in the world.* And yet, I knew I'd fight like hell to keep her in my life.

Her finger brushed over the scar on my chest, and then she kissed it softly. That small gesture had my body coming alive again, ready to go for round two. But then she jumped up. "Come on." Reaching down for my hand, she said, "We haven't gone skinny dipping in ages."

I shook my head, releasing a chuckle. "Skinny dipping? You think I would have taken this long to be with you if I'd ever seen you naked?"

I let her pull me up, and then gazed down at her, waiting, trying to keep eye contact when she was only in her panties.

She shrugged. "Whatever, you saw me in my underwear."

She was right. "And it was torture."

Her sexy grin grew, then she wrapped her arms around me, pulling me in to keep her warm. "Good! Now let's go before I change my mind."

I liked the ocean; Ava loved it. So, of course, I didn't say no. "One quick dip and then home...to a hot shower and bed."

"Mmm. I like that." She took off, running.

I followed, catching her before she reached the water's edge. Swooping her up, I carried her into the ocean. We held each other as the chilling waves crashed over us, a symbol of the outside forces that threatened us being together. But I wouldn't let that happen. *Ava is mine. Now and forever.* But I prayed I wouldn't lose the family over it. *I can't lose them either.*

Back at my place, we rushed across the wood floor to my bedroom, our hair still damp. We dropped our stuff in front of the bed, ready to jump into the shower.

"Let me grab some new towels, and I'll meet you in there," I told her.

Her phone buzzed, and she snatched it from the pile on the floor. "Oh, shoot, I forgot to text Gunnar that everything was okay." She laughed.

"Let him sweat it out." I grinned and went to get the

towels while Ava dropped her phone and headed for the bathroom.

Mere seconds later, I returned with the towels. Ava's phone had slipped from the pile and I almost stepped on it. Picking it up, I saw there was a new text on the screen, a preview. But it wasn't Gunnar. I stared in confusion at the screen. My chest tightened as I read the first words: *I'm sorry to bother you, but have you told Alex yet? I don't think I can...* The rest of the message was cut off. Her phone was likely locked, but as my heart pounded frantically in my chest, my eyes moved to the name on the message: *Maggie.* "What the fuck?" My brain raced, my breath labored, heat suffusing my whole body. *This can't be right.* Why the hell was Ava messaging with my mother...and why would she keep it a secret from me?

Chapter Twenty-Nine

Ava

I pulled the only towel off the rack and wrapped it around me after a speedy rinse off from being in the ocean. Alex never showed up to get in with me let alone bring the towels he mentioned. My first thought was that he got a work call, but after him being late and our argument, I hoped it wasn't that.

My hair dripping, I opened the door to the bathroom and saw him sitting on the bed with his back to me. "Alex?"

He didn't answer, didn't move.

My underwear was still damp and on his floor, so I grabbed the leggings I wore as I passed the pile and headed over to him. "What happened?" I asked as I came up beside him. My heart stopped when he turned to glare at me, and I saw he was holding my phone.

"What the hell's going on, Ava?" His voice was deep, cold, a tone he'd never used with me before.

"What do you mean?" Of course I was pretty sure, so playing dumb tasted horrible on my tongue, but I had to be sure.

"Why is my mother texting you?" His dark eyes held mine, unblinking.

A chill ran over me, partially because I was still in a towel but mostly because I was exposed, caught in my deception. "I can explain…" My breathing labored, and my eyes stung with threatening tears. I held them back because that wouldn't be fair to him. "Just let me put my clothes on, please." I turned and heard his deep sigh at my back as I put on my leggings, found my shirt, and quickly pulled it over my head.

The moment I turned, he rose from the bed. "Dammit, Ava! What the fuck were you thinking? You saw how it affected me? You were there." He closed the distance between us and peered down at me. "Five seconds in my mother's presence broke me, and you still— what? Did you reach out to her, think you could fix me or something?"

My heart pounded in my chest, fear that if he was this angry at the assumption we'd only recently connected, how would he react to the real truth? "I'm afraid that's not exactly what happened."

He roughed a hand through his hair. "I don't have the patience for these games, Ava. You obviously went behind my back. You're exchanging texts with my mother. Why?"

I nodded to the bed. "Can we sit?"

His hands on his hips, he shook his head. "Just tell me."

I drew in a deep breath and began. "I first met your mother at your dad's funeral." I winced, waiting for his reaction.

"You've got to be fucking kidding me," he growled, pacing away from me over to his dresser.

Strangely, I took that moment to note he didn't have any pictures in his room of his parents, of them as a family growing up, no memories at all. I didn't recall seeing them elsewhere either. It broke my heart how much pain his family had caused him, and I made it worse. "I'm sorry. She approached me," I said defensively. "What was I supposed to do?"

He shook his head, as if he didn't have an answer for that.

We stared at each other for long moments before he said, "What did she say?"

"She wanted to thank me... She knew about me already, about Sammy, our fam—"

"How, dammit!"

Nervously, I locked my fingers together and explained how she'd learned bits and pieces from social media, how she'd found out different things about Alex and his life, how she knew we'd been taking care of him, considered him part of our family. "She also knew I lived in Vegas, and since she did too..."

"No..." He dragged a hand down his jaw. "Please, don't tell me you're...friends?" He said the word like it disgusted him.

"No, we're not—"

"Then what? Why was she texting you? What the hell was she talking about? And how could you not tell me?"

Every word dripped with pain that was like a knife to my gut. But I deserved it.

Hesitantly, I moved over to him by the dresser. Putting a hand on his arm, I said gently, "First, you should know that when I met with her in Vegas, she was living in a homeless shelter."

The hard edges of Alex's face softened, his eyes filled with emotion but he didn't speak, so I continued.

"She'd been clean for quite a while but had a setback and pretty much lost everything. She would show up at the food pantry I volunteered at, and we'd chat a little, mostly about her situation. I only wanted to help her,

Alex. But then she started asking questions about you, wanting to learn more about your life."

Alex pulled his hand from mine. His chest rose and fell quickly and in a strained whisper, he said, "All this time... Why didn't you just tell me?"

"She begged me not to. She was ashamed...of what she's done, of what her life became. And she didn't want you to have any more pain because of her."

"And yet here we goddamn are..." He moved past me, headed out of the room.

"What are you doing?" I said, following him.

"I need a drink." He went into the kitchen, pulled out a bottle of bourbon, and poured a healthy portion before slugging the whole thing down.

My heart broke as I watched his back, waiting for him to turn back around.

"So, what else?" he asked without turning to face me.

Hesitantly, I spoke. "I know I should have told you... but I was torn. You never wanted to talk about her, so I figured it was better you didn't know, especially since she didn't want me to. But she's doing so much better now, has a job, a place... She even started volunteering at the food pantry. Then I moved back home. I didn't think I'd see her again."

He turned, leaned against the counter. "Then we saw

her in Vegas. You could have said something right then. Or any time after."

The disapproving look on his face cut to my core, and I could no longer fight the tears. My throat clogged and moisture gathered in my lashes. "I'm sorry, Alex. I was going to tell you but things with us have been—"

"What? Complicated?"

"Well, yes, but I was going to say wonderful...and I was afraid of how you'd react, of what it would do to us."

"Looks like you were fucking right, then," he said with a coldness that struck fear in me.

"Alex—"

"I want you to go."

My breath caught, and I stared at him, my heart hanging in the balance. The silence lingered as I grappled with what to say, what to do. *What does this mean?*

Alex's features transformed from anger to sadness, something even harder to witness. "I can't do this, Ava. You knew..." He shook his head. "Now you've forced me into a place I don't want to be, don't you see?"

"I'm sorry. Can't we—" I cut myself off at seeing his jaw clench. There was no point. I'd ruined everything. Leaving him in the kitchen, I returned to the bedroom to quickly gather my things. At his front door, I swiped at my wet cheeks. "You might want me gone, and you might not want to face your past, but your mother isn't a monster.

And she's not your father either. She's human. She had a problem. A disease. And she's worked hard to change. Maybe you still don't want her in your life, but hiding from your pain is never going to make you feel whole." With that, I walked out the door. I stalled in the hallway, saying a silent prayer that he'd come after me, say he forgave me and still loved me. But the door remained closed, and I knew my heart would never recover without him.

Chapter Thirty

Alex

I leaned back on my couch, staring up at nothing, music barely audible coming from the speakers in the ceiling. I didn't know what time it was or how long I'd been there. Almost immediately after coming home from work, that was where I landed—with a halfway decent bottle of whiskey. I had a purpose for this drinking session, and I wasn't about to waste the good stuff on it.

I swung my legs back to the ground and sat up, surveying the mess I'd made on the coffee table. Pushing aside the files I'd hoped to work on, I peered down at the family photo I hadn't laid eyes on in years. Two years ago, when I'd cleaned out my father's house, the house I grew up in, I sold most everything. But at Sammy and Ava's convincing, I'd kept a small amount of photos.

Picking up the photo, I noted how detached I felt from that moment. It was taken not long before the accident. We looked like any other normal family. But we never were. My chest tightened, anger bubbling up from my gut. This was why I didn't want to think about my past, about my mother. And Ava had to go and bring it right to my doorstep. *Ava...* I didn't want to think about her either. Couldn't even click on the dozens of text messages and voicemails she'd left me. Still, I ached for her, even despite my anger.

I let the photo fall back to the coffee table, and then as if on cue, my doorbell rang. I'd ordered food, but I knew it wasn't that since the guy had already texted he'd left my dinner on the mat ten minutes ago.

Ignoring it, I grabbed the whiskey bottle and took another long pull. After a few more knocks and rings, I heard the door opening and then footsteps.

"What the hell, man," Sammy said, coming from the door.

I didn't bother looking over, just waited as he walked behind me, rounded the couch, then sat down on the chair to my right. "Your fucking dinner?" he said, slapping the bag down on the coffee table.

"I'm not hungry. You eat it." I took another drink and

avoided eye contact. Sammy was a lot more in touch with his feelings than I was, and he was always pressing me to talk about shit I didn't want to.

He tore open the bag and pulled out my roast beef sandwich. "Since you freaking stood me up, I will." He unwrapped the sandwich, took half out, and jammed it into his mouth for a big bite. "But I'll save you the other half in case you change your mind." Even pissed, he was still a caring person. *Just like his sister.* I brushed the thought away.

Sammy's mouth was still full when he re-wrapped the rest of the sandwich while he chewed.

After a few minutes of silence—save for Sammy's aggressive eating—he said, "Well...what the hell happened to our cigar night?"

I knew I'd screwed him since it wasn't easy for him to leave Cass and Dax.

I sighed. "Sorry, man... Some shit happened." I finally looked at him, and he watched me carefully.

"It's a woman. What happened? That Lauren chick, right?"

"Let it go, bro." I shook my head and grabbed the other half of the sandwich, knowing I needed to sober up before I said some stupid shit.

"You blow cigar night and don't even answer my texts

or calls, and I'm supposed to drop it?" He shook his head. "No screw that."

I took a bite of the sandwich, deciding what if anything I should say. Sammy would needle me until I broke, or we fought.

"Never seen you like this, brother, so I know it has to be a woman."

"How do you figure?" I asked lamely.

"Because this is exactly what I was like when Cass tried to dump me...remember?" He grinned, and I knew it was because he'd ultimately won her back. This was totally different.

I wasn't ready to tell him everything, so I said, "She kept something from me." Not exactly a lie.

"Damn, sorry. Must have been a hell of a thing if you're this messed up." His hands froze with the sandwich poised in front of his lips. "She have a boyfriend or something?"

I opened my mouth but stuffed it with another bite instead.

"Whatever," he said under his breath. He set the roast beef down, wiped his hands on his jeans, then reached across the coffee table. "Whoa... Have I seen this picture? Look at you." He chuckled, but it quickly died on his lips when he saw my reaction.

"You want something to drink?" I asked.

"No thanks." He dropped the photo in front of me. "What's going on? What's all this about?"

I could hear the frustration in his voice, but I knew I couldn't tell him part of the story. It was all or nothing. My head was still spinning, but I also still had a healthy dose of bitterness swirling in my gut. "I'm sorry about tonight. I'll make it up to you."

Sammy let out a sigh and shook his head. "You know, I'm getting tired of this shit. You always putting up a damn wall, acting like we're not fucking brothers."

His words cut me deep. I could see the hurt on his face, and I scrambled for the right words as he continued.

"Bro, you've been right with me through the hardest damn times of my life, helped me through them, but you never let me return the favor."

Trying to take some of the edge off, I said, "So, this is about you?"

"Damn right it is." He wasn't laughing, though. "You know what. I'm just gonna fuckin' go." He stood and paced toward the door.

"It was your sister," I blurted.

I heard his footsteps stop, and I turned to look at him.

"What do you mean my sister? What about Ava?"

Our gazes locked for a few beats, and in his I could have sworn I already saw anger building up. Almost as if he'd seen this coming a mile away. "The woman I've been seeing. The woman who kept something from me... It was Ava...not Lauren."

His mouth fell open, but no words came for several seconds. "I... You screwing with me? Because it's not—"

"It's the truth. But it's not what you think. Ava and I—"

"Not what I think!" He ran a hand over his jaw. "How the hell do you know what I think when you never even gave me a chance to understand? God damn, Alex. You and Ava?" His head swiveled around like he was looking for answers or like she'd pop out from a room somewhere. "When— How—" He shook his head.

"None of it matters because we're not together anymore."

"None of it matters? Are you fucking crazy?" He backed away to the door. "I don't know if I'm more pissed you were doing my sister behind my back or that you never trust me enough to tell me a goddamn thing. Jesus, Alex."

I stood and paced toward him as he reached the door. "I know. I'm sorry. I messed everything up."

"And you're going to fix it, whatever you do." He pointed at me. "And don't think you're taking the coward way out. You damn well better be at family dinner to face this shit you created!" Then he walked out, slamming the door behind him.

Chapter Thirty-One

Ava

The table was set beautifully as usual, and when I carried over Mom's famous cheddar mash potatoes and placed them on the trivet, my heart sank. Those were Alex's favorite, so my mom often made sure to include them when she knew he was coming to family dinner. But I didn't see him showing up on this night. He'd made it clear he didn't want to see or hear from me, so I couldn't imagine him coming. Still, his regular place was set and as I stared at it, my eyes watered over. I understood he was hurt, but to close me out was painful.

"I'm sorry Gunnar couldn't make it," Mom said, setting a basket of rolls on the table.

"He's in Vegas, visiting his sister." I kept my face

turned away, but her quiet pause had me sneaking a peek at her.

Mom was looking at the clock on the wall. "I'm surprised Alex isn't here yet. Maybe he's not coming?"

She glanced my way, and I shrugged and pretended to brush some crumbs off the table and into my hand.

"He'll be here," Sammy said, coming from the kitchen, his voice deep and edgy. He'd been a grump since the moment he, Cass, and Dax arrived, and much of it seemed to be directed at me. I hadn't seen him act this way since the time I borrowed his car when I'd only had my learner's permit, and then dented the front fender on a trash can.

My stomach dropped at his words. Had he spoken to Alex in the last few days? If he knew, which I doubted, why would he be so insistent that Alex would be here? I waited for him to look my way, and when he did, his eyes narrowed.

"Do you know any reason he wouldn't be here?" Sammy said to me, his gaze unwavering.

My heart jumped into my throat. When I opened my mouth to say who knew what, Dax ran in, followed by Cass.

"Honey, can you take Dax to wash his hands, please?"

I caught a glimpse of Sammy's jaw clenching before he turned to his son and took his hand. "Come on, buddy."

"I'm sitting next to Uncle Alex, right?"

I didn't hear Sammy's answer as the door to the bathroom closed.

"We can't wait much longer," Mom said. "The food will get cold. Honey, can you grab your dad from the den?"

I nodded and headed down the hall, my shoulders feeling heavy with the weight that I'd already changed everything. I'd ruined family dinner, Alex's relationship with my parents, with Sammy, and they didn't even know it...yet.

I stood in the doorway to my dad's den. Glasses perched on the edge of his nose, he was reading a magazine, something you rarely saw people do unless they were in a doctor's office. It made me smile. And have some hope. My parents were good, smart people. I had to believe they wouldn't hold any of this against Alex. Even if they didn't, it still felt like Alex was pulling away. Maybe he no longer felt like this was his home.

"Dad," I croaked out, startled at the sound of my own raspy voice.

Dad looked up, saw my face, and rose.

"Dinner's ready," I said, trying to hang on to my composure. Just looking at my dad when I was upset could cause the dam to break.

"And it looks that bad?" he said with a chuckle,

coming over to me. He slipped an arm around my shoulders. "You all right, honey?"

Shit.

"Yeah," I said quickly.

"Don't tell me you miss him already?"

My heart skipped a beat, eyes widening. "What?"

"Gunnar. Just thought you might be having trouble in the new place without him."

"Oh..." I let out a sigh.

"But he's coming back soon, right?" He head-gestured to the hall, and we started walking.

"Yeah, soon..." When I thought about it, he was right. I did need Gunnar. He'd offered to come home early when I told him what happened, but I made him promise not to cut his family time short.

We all took our seats at the table and began filling up our plates. I couldn't help but eye the empty spot where Alex was supposed to be. Maybe he just needed some time... The thought of us not being together was hard enough to bear, but there was no way I could accept him not being part of our family.

Moments later, I heard the door open, and my heart stuttered against my ribs. My eyes were glued to the doorway as his footsteps drew closer. When he came around the corner, my mother jumped up to greet him.

She wrapped him in a hug, and his eyes cut to mine

over her shoulder. I swallowed back the lump in my throat, seeing the pain in his eyes. Mom's smile when she pulled back was like salt in the wound. They really did love him like a son, and I couldn't take that away from any of them. Somehow I would make it right.

"I can't stay," Alex said quickly. His eyes panned around the table as he held up a bag. "I'm just dropping off dessert."

I watched as his eyes darted to Sammy and then back to my mom.

"You didn't have to go to the trouble," she said, taking the bag from his hands.

"Yes he did," Sammy blurted.

All eyes went to Sammy.

"Babe," Cass said tightly.

"What? He gets here late and then doesn't even stay..." Sammy dug into the cheddar mash potatoes, taking a huge scoop over to his plate. Then began eating as if we weren't all questioning his behavior.

"Ignore him," Mom said, patting the lapel of Alex's suit jacket. "Thank you for bringing dessert. But listen, did you call Uncle Jo yet?"

Alex winced. "I'm sorry I haven't had a chance..."

Sammy huffed under his breath. Dad, oblivious to the tension, just continued to eat his dinner.

"It's all right, but please do it soon. He's not trying to

get money from you. He says he just wants advice on whether or not it's a good investment."

Alex smiled down at my mother, but I could see how forced it was. He was in pain and needed his family, and because of me he couldn't let them comfort him. "I promise. I'll call him next week." He nodded, then added, "Now get back to your dinner. I'm going to head back out." Without looking at anyone but my mom, he turned to go.

As I watched him walk away, my heart cracked, but I fought the emotion. I couldn't fall apart at the table. I wasn't ready to explain things just yet. I sensed myself slipping into despair as I reached for my water and took a sip. Then I felt Cass's hand on my other arm under the table. She gave it a gentle squeeze, and I turned to her. She showed me a soft, knowing look. *She knows, which means Sammy knows.* So, my brother was pissed at me and clearly Alex, too, but Cass had no judgment on her face, and that was the only thing keeping me from losing it. I gave her a grateful smile, then spent the rest of the dinner in my head, trying to figure out how the hell I was going to make things right.

Chapter Thirty-Two

Alex

I stood over the desk of one of my analysts as he frantically rummaged through piles of paper, looking for the contract I requested an hour ago. It wasn't urgent but his incompetence coupled with my mood at this late hour of the evening had me glaring at him. I thought working late would take my mind off Ava, but nothing seemed to do that. "This shit is not going to fly, Corbin."

"I know. I don't know what the hell happened to it." He stood and looked over at the one other analyst still working. Sheryl just shrugged and quickly glanced away—self-preservation I couldn't blame her for.

Just then my phone vibrated in my pocket, and I

pulled it out to find a text alert from Gunnar. The last few texts that came from Ava I couldn't even find the strength to open. That plus the fact that Gunnar never texted me had my heart racing and a knot forming in my gut.

I tapped into the message as Corbin muttered more lame excuses.

Gunnar: *Hey, Mr. Big Shot. I hope you see this message because I'm gonna call you in 5 minutes, and if you don't answer your goddamn phone, I'm going to fly back from Vegas and kick your ass. This is about Ava, and it's important.*

"Shit."

Whatever Corbin was saying didn't matter at the moment. Not even the damn contract mattered as I sped-walked down the hallway, ignoring Corbin calling my name.

By the time I stepped into my office and closed the door behind me, the phone was already ringing, even though it had only been three minutes.

"Alex Bannister."

"Don't answer my fucking call like you didn't know it was me."

"Sorry, habit." I leaned against my desk and ran a hand through my hair. "Why are you calling, Gunnar? Did something happen to Ava?"

"Not yet."

His accusing tone confused and startled me. I pushed off the desk, then paced to the window and looked out into the night, as if there were some security for me there. "What the hell are you talking about? What happened?"

"Look, I don't feel good about any of this. I don't even know if I should've called you, but I was on the phone with Ava tonight, and she's incredibly wasted. She said her and our friend Greta were going to meet at O'Grady's Pub tonight."

I sighed, relieved it wasn't something serious but also annoyed I had to hear this. "Look, Gunnar, I'm sorry you're not there to babysit Ava while she tries to drink away her guilt, but she's with a friend. What do you need me for?"

"That's the thing. Ava was going on and on about how much she missed you, and how she wishes she could go back to before you guys were together. Then that sent her off on a whole tangent about how much she misses dancing too..."

Growing impatient, I said, "Yeah, so? Get to the point."

"You know how they have karaoke night at O'Grady's? Well, tonight they're doing something different. They're having amateur stripper pole night, and Ava's going...*to enter!*"

Instantly, I was thrown back to the days of beating asses on Ava's behalf. Ava could always handle herself, but I could never control my feelings of jealousy and protectiveness. But this was different. If she was drunk...and taking off her clothes. What was she thinking? *Obviously, they won't be naked, but still...* "Why didn't you stop her!" I blurted.

"Don't yell at me. This is all your fault."

"My fault?" I huffed out a breath. "I've gotta go."

"What are you going to do?"

"Whatever I have to," I said, rushing to my desk and grabbing my keys. I tapped an end to the call without another word to him.

"Dammit, Ava!"

By the time I got to the bar, it was packed house. Twin sisters held the stage, wearing booty shorts and bikini tops and executing the most awkward pole dancing I'd ever seen. The guy's cat-calling didn't seem to mind. I could only imagine what they'd do when a professional dancer like Ava took the stage.

Working my way through the crowds, I scanned every corner of the place for Ava and didn't see her. As a couple more dancers came and went, I began to calm down. Maybe she changed her mind and left... I thought about texting her, but I couldn't bring myself to do it. At that point, it wasn't just the lying—it was Sammy's reaction, the awkward family dinner moment...exactly what I was afraid would happen.

I went to the bar and ordered a bourbon and just as the bartender set it down in front of me, the MC said Ava's name. I clenched my jaw as my heart slammed in my chest.

"Fuck," I whispered to myself as Ava took the stage wearing what I thought I recognized as one of her old performance costumes. Two piece, tight-fitting, black and silver top with spaghetti straps and fringe and a matching short skirt. The crowd went wild but Ava was in character, unsmiling, seductive.

I pushed through the guys trying to jockey for the front but stopped short, mesmerized by her movement. I'd always loved watching her dance, could never take my eyes off her. *God, she's amazing.* My heart ached with how much I missed her. The anger was still there, though, fighting to keep its place at the forefront of my mind.

"Damn, now that's what I call a woman," a guy said to his friend.

This was going to end badly for everyone if I didn't get Ava off that stage. Especially if a single comment had my blood boiling. I pushed between the guy and his friend with a little too much force.

"Hey, watch it!" the guy's friend said.

Ava danced her way over to the pole, and I held some

relief that her experience and training never involved poles. Then she grabbed it, swirled around it before doing a body wave against it. *Shit.* Apparently, I didn't know everything there was to know about Ava.

The crowd cheered, but Ava's face never changed, almost like she hadn't heard them, was lost in the music.

I was almost to the front when another guy leaned up toward the stage and was saying something to her. I rushed up behind him. "Back off!"

Ava's eyes met mine and then widened. I figured she'd stop when she saw me, but she just kept dancing.

"What are you security?" the guy said sarcastically.

"I'm *her* security, and if you don't back the fuck off, you'll be shitting out your teeth."

Frozen for a few seconds, he seemed to be contemplating how serious I was. Then he raised his hands and backed away.

Taking a couple steps to the right, I positioned myself right under Ava and said, "Let's go!"

Pausing her moves, she glanced down at me with a narrowed gaze.

Boos and rants came from behind me, but I still held my hand up to her.

"Let her dance!" yelled someone.

Ava sauntered to the other side of the pole, dancing and looking out at the crowd, who began cheering again.

Losing patience, I said loud enough that she would hear me. "You've got two seconds to get your ass down here before I come up there and throw you over my shoulder." Then I took my coat off and held my hand out again.

With fire in her eyes, she sighed, took my hand and jumped down from the stage. I threw my coat over her shoulders and guided her from behind around the crowd instead of through, ignoring the boos following us.

"What do you want, Alex!" she threw over her shoulder.

I ignored her until we got outside, then took her hand and dragged her down the street.

"Wait! Where the hell are we going?!"

"I'm taking you home."

Chapter Thirty-Three

Ava

I slammed the car door and bolted toward my apartment, completely aware that Alex would follow. His heavy footsteps stayed behind me the whole way. He'd make sure I got in the door, then he would leave.

We'd been silent the entire way home, and I had flashbacks of being a brooding teenager with two overbearing big brothers, who always thought they knew what was best for me. I'd hated it back then, but this... I couldn't even process the emotions whirling through me. He didn't want anything to do with me, and yet he stepped back in to treat me like a child?

By the time I got the key into the door, I felt Alex at

my back. I hesitated a beat, trying to parse the flood of emotions at his close proximity. When he stood fast as I opened the door, I said under my breath, "I don't remember inviting you in."

He ignored my statement, pushing in behind me, then shutting the door as I paced to the kitchen.

Opening the fridge, I was reminded that I had finished off the last bottle of cheap wine before I left.

Dammit.

"Haven't you had enough to drink?"

His sarcasm fueled my anger and humiliation, and I shot him a glare. "Someone killed my buzz."

Alex leaned back against the counter, folded his arms, and glared right back. I saw the twitch of his jaw as he clenched it.

"Why are you even still here? I thought you wanted nothing to do with me?"

He ran a hand through his hair. "Despite what's going on between us, I had to make sure you were okay and didn't do anything...*stupid.*"

Maybe it was stupid, but I wasn't about to admit that to him or let on how humiliated I was, so I moved across the kitchen and went into the living room. "Well, I'm fine now, so you can see yourself out." I didn't know what hurt more: that Alex had ignored me for days or that when he finally surfaced it was in "big brother" mode.

A moment later, Alex walked through the living room and right toward the front door.

I practically gasped in anger. Yes, I had told him to go, but... *I can't believe he's actually going to leave.* I rushed across the room and slammed the door shut when he only had it a foot open. "You coward!"

He spun to face me, pointing his dark gaze down at me, but I didn't waver, and I didn't take my palm off the door.

"Me? You're the one who was too afraid to tell me the truth, and then instead of facing what you did, you try to drink your guilt away."

My mouth flew open. "No! You don't get to say that when I tried to face what I did, but you shut me out. And I wasn't drinking my guilt away. I was trying to drink *you* away."

His eyes widened for a beat before he caught himself. "Yeah, well next time do it in the privacy of your own home." His hand still on the knob, he pulled but not hard enough. He was strong enough to rip the damn door from the hinges if he wanted to, so he could certainly over power me. But I knew he wouldn't, so I didn't budge.

"Dammit, Alex, just talk to me. I'll take whatever you dish out. Cuss me out, scream at me. I deserve it." I knew I'd never be able to move forward with his silence, with the uncertainty of his forgiveness. But somehow, we at least had to get back to the way things were...*before us.*

His chest heaved deeply as he stared down at me, his anger apparent, even though I could see him holding it back. I took my hand from the door and placed it on his chest, my own heart stuttering. "You can walk out that door and never look back, but I'm not letting you leave until you talk to me. Tell me you hate me, that you never want to see me again." My heart racing, I paused to catch my breath. "Say it, Alex!" I yelled.

Alex grabbed my wrist tightly, his mouth pursed. "This is what you want?!" He paced me backward.

"Yes!" I said, breathlessly but with no fear of him hurting me.

"I had everything in my life under control, and you destroyed that!" He stopped in the middle of the living room and yanked me against his chest. "You went behind my back, you lied, and you ruined us, Ava!"

"I know," I barely got out, my throat closing up. "I'm sorry."

"Even if I could ever trust you again... Now when I see you, I think of—" He turned his face away.

Risking his anger escalating, I said, "You can't run from your memories, from her, forever."

He returned his gaze to me but didn't speak.

"And as much as your words say otherwise, you can't

run from me, Alex. We will always be a part of each other's lives. I will not let you run from our family either."

He released my wrist and stepped back. "Watch me."

When he turned to leave I rushed around him, put both hands on his chest, stopping him. "No."

"Move, Ava."

"No!" He was either going to talk this out with me or tell me once and for all it was over. He'd yet to say those exact words, and I prayed that he wouldn't. Our eyes were locked in a silent battle for what felt like minutes but was probably only seconds before I reached up and touched his cheek.

Then in an instant, he grabbed my shoulders, hard. I thought he was going to shove me out of the way but instead, he crashed his mouth down on to mine. It was an angry but desperate kiss, his mouth devouring mine as he continued to grip my shoulders.

I took it all, grateful for the connection, prepared to have him however he was willing to give. When he finally tore his mouth from mine and gazed at me, I saw the anger was still there. Anger mixed with pain. He panted, his lips mere inches from mine, then slowly, I reached for his belt. He held my stare as I undid it but as soon as I got the first button undone, he shoved my hand away, then yanked down the strap of my top. It didn't take much to get me naked, given the outfit I'd been wearing. When I stood before him, his eyes feasted on me before his lips began tasting inch after inch of my body like I was his last meal, like it was the last time he would get to touch me.

My hands went to his hair, and I pulled his mouth back to mine. We kissed frantically before he moved us toward the back of the couch. Turning me around, he pressed up against me until I was wedged between him and the couch. I didn't know if it was about control or him no longer wanting to look into my eyes, but I didn't care. All I wanted was to be with him. I heard his clothes hit the floor, and seconds later, he was inside me. It was fast and rough and erotic, and when I screamed out his name as we both fell over the edge of ecstasy, my eyes watered with the uncertainty of this being *goodbye*.

As I calmed my breathing, my heart hanging in the balance, Alex surprised me by lifting me into his arms. He carried me to my bedroom, and there we made slow, sweet love all night long. We didn't speak after, and I fell asleep in his arms, my head against his chest.

But when I woke up sometime before dawn, the space next to me was cold. And Alex was gone.

Chapter Thirty-Four

Alex

I sat across from the nurses' station, holding a to-go cup of coffee and pretending not to notice the two young ladies at the counter eyeing me. It looked like one of them might have even snapped a pic of me, but I couldn't be sure. The old me would have strolled over and secured at least one of their numbers. But I was in no mood to flirt, let alone even think about women.

One of the older nurses walked up, and the two girls separated. "Jill, Mr. Evers is specifically asking for you again."

The one with the phone slid it onto the desk and said, "I'll check on him."

When she walked off, the older woman turned to me. "Alex, right?"

As soon as she said it, I recognized her as Gayle, a charge nurse that Sue had introduced me to a while back.

I stood and moved to the counter. "Yes, how are you, Gayle?"

The slight blush in her cheeks told me she appreciated I'd remembered, especially since I didn't see a name tag on her.

"Did someone page Sue for you?"

"I'm right here, Gayle," Sue said, walking up behind me.

Her hand landed on my back, and when I turned, she gave me the reassuring smile I'd apparently come there for. Or, at least that was one of the reasons. As if she'd been expecting me, she said, "Come on. Let's go to the lounge. I have a few minutes."

I nodded to Gayle and then followed Sue down the hallway.

Handing her the to-go cup when I fell in line beside her, I said, "Your favorite but unfortunately probably cold by now."

"I'll pop it into the microwave before we sit."

I hadn't planned on going there that afternoon, just got in my car after a lunch meeting and found myself driving toward the hospital. But Sue didn't even ask me what I wanted.

At the lounge, she led us over to a couple of chairs in a quiet corner, then walked over to a microwave on a cart. When she returned and took the seat across from me, panic shot through my system. What could I possibly say to this woman that wouldn't have her disappointed in me? I supposed guilt had led me there, but it was trepidation that had dried my mouth right up.

As if we had all the time in the world, she sipped her coffee and watched me. "Mmm, just what I needed. Thank you."

"You're welcome." I grinned and after a moment I said, "I spoke to Jo last night."

Setting the cup on the small table, she said, "Oh, good. Were you able to help him?"

I nodded. "The information he sent me was solid, but I'm just not sure with his limited income if he should risk it."

"Then I'm guessing that's exactly what JoJo will do." She laughed. "Thank you for doing that."

I couldn't help but laugh too. "Yeah, of course." But the look on her face had me pausing, my pulse quickening. Silence hung in the air, and as usual Sue knew exactly what the score was.

"I still have a few more minutes, so why don't you tell me why you're really here, Alex."

My mouth parted, but I couldn't find the words, wasn't sure how to start this thing.

She leaned over, put her hand on mine as it rested on my knee. "Whatever it is, it's all right...you know?"

Her concern, her sheer acceptance of me, something she'd always done, felt achingly undeserving. I'd never expected a thing from the Steadmans, never even asked for anything. But they continued to give and be there for me. Even when I wasn't the easiest person to get along with. Part of me wanted them to disown me for what I'd done, but a bigger part of me wanted to unburden myself and beg forgiveness.

Pulling my hand from beneath hers, I drew in a breath and sighed. "I need to tell you something. I, uh... I've kept something from you." It dawned on me briefly that maybe I should have talked to Ava, or at least given her a heads up, but I didn't care anymore. I didn't owe her that now after what she'd done. Even after last night, which was too complicated to process, I wasn't sure how we could move forward.

Her expression didn't waver as she waited.

I ran a hand through my hair. "I don't know how to say this, but I want you to know that what happened, what I've done, is all my fault. No one else's. I'm the one who messed everything up, so please remember that." It was a small consolation for Ava but the truth nonetheless.

She gave me a tight smile, folded her arms across her chest. "Okay..."

I glanced around the room before looking her in the eyes again. "I was seeing someone...and well, it didn't work out. But the thing is, I never should have been seeing her." I shook my head at how ridiculous I was being. I should have taken the band-aid approach. "Shit, this is... She—"

"Alex..." She scooted her chair closer to me and leaned in. "I'm sorry. I know how much Ava means to you, but are you sure—"

"What?" My loud voice had her brows raising. "I'm sorry but what are you saying?"

She gave me one of those self-assured motherly looks. "Please, you think I didn't see how you two have been all these years? I'm surprised it took you this long to get together."

My jaw dropped as she spoke. "Why didn't you say anything?"

"Why didn't you?" She tilted her head. "You two didn't want anyone to know so...I figured I'd wait until you were ready. I also figured something had happened between you two after the dinner the other night."

My eyes pleaded for forgiveness. "I'm sorry. I don't know what else to say."

"Except that you love her, right?"

Giving her a tight smile, I replied, "I've always loved Ava."

She let a little chuckle out. "But now you're *in love* with her."

I nodded even though it wasn't a question.

"So, you're here... You might as well tell me all of it. What happened?"

I told her as quickly and painlessly as I could about Ava connecting with my mother behind my back, about our run-in while in Vegas, and about our fight. Then I said, "I feel like I can't trust her anymore."

She shook her head. "Do you really believe that, Alex? Or are you just hurt and angry because you feel like you can't hide from this anymore?"

My mouth pursed, but I didn't answer. We both knew.

She sighed. "Listen, I don't condone what she did. But what she did was for you...because she loves you and because she knew you'd always have this fracture in your heart if you didn't face your past. I'm not asking you to move on like nothing happened. But, honey, you've always had this piece of you that you guarded no matter how hard we all tried. A part of you that you...wouldn't let us love. How can she love you completely if you are always holding something back?"

Sue was the one person I'd felt secure speaking to, and

I didn't think that had changed so I said, "I know. And I've thought a lot about it. I'm not blaming it all on her. But everything's different now."

"She messed up. But what you two have is too special, too strong to throw away." She stared at me, and when I didn't respond, she continued, "The question is, are you going to keep running from your past or acknowledge it? Because staying away from Ava isn't going to make this go away. If and when you're ready to deal with it, it's Ava who's going to help you through it."

I shook my head and chuckled. "Damn, you are one wise woman."

"I know." She glanced at her watch. "And unfortunately, I need to get back."

We both rose, and she gave me a hug. I held on longer than usual, but she let me linger until I was ready to pull away. Showing me one of those sweet smiles, she said, "Feel better?"

"Yeah...I actually do." I bent and kissed her on the cheek. "Thank you."

"I love you."

"I love you too."

Chapter Thirty-Five

Ava

Squatting in front of my dad's raised-up car, I pushed the pan back under the engine. "Is that far enough?" I called over my shoulder.

"You tell me," he replied.

I left it there and said, "Yeah, I guess that's right."

"No, a little bit farther, honey."

Thanks.

I pushed it a few more inches, and he said, "Right there. Now you're gonna have to really get under there like I showed you."

"Really, Dad? Can't you just pay someone to change your oil?"

"Sure I could. But you said you wanted to talk, right? We haven't done anything like this in a long time."

"Yeah, there's a reason for that. Because I'm not fifteen anymore."

"Well, you have a car, and you need to learn how to change your oil."

Instead of telling him I had absolutely no intention of ever changing my oil by myself, I ducked back under there and looked for the cap. Growing up, I couldn't get out of all the stuff Dad always tried to teach me, things he'd said I needed to know to survive on my own. But if I were being honest, I did like the special time with him, since he and Sammy were always doing things together. "We have had some great talks doing stuff like this, Dad, but I didn't have this in mind when I came here."

"Think of it as helping me out. Now, remember to pull your hand away quickly so it doesn't get too much oil on it."

"Too late." I came out from under the car and my dad had a rag waiting for me.

As I wiped the oil off my hands, he said, "So, you're having boy trouble, huh?"

Maybe this was a mistake. "Dad, this isn't about some boy I'm dating on the football team. This is serious."

"So, what did he do?"

As I watched the oil drip into the pan, I cringed. "It wasn't him. It was me."

Dad helped me to my feet. "What? My perfect little angel did something wrong?" The humor in his voice warmed my heart, even though this conversation was going nowhere fast.

"Yes, Dad, I screwed up."

"Did you apologize?"

Tilting my head, I gave him the same look from when I was a teenager.

His mouth made an exaggerated O as he said, "Oh...I see." He took the rag from my hand and gave me one of his tight smiles. "So, this is bigger than an apology?"

"It is."

"Then I guess you need to ask yourself if this guy is worth it. And if he is, then you need to fix it."

"That's the trouble. I don't know how to fix it."

He stared at me a moment and then said, "Remember that time you and Sammy took a whole apple pie from the bake sale without paying for it?"

I leaned against the side of the car. "This is hardly the same thing, Dad. We didn't really hurt anyone, and we ended up paying for it. But what I've done... I really hurt his feelings and broke his trust and probably put him in a bad situation."

He nodded, and I could see in his eyes he wanted to

help. But then he said, "You didn't just pay for it. Don't you remember?"

I remembered, but I still didn't see the correlation. "Yes, but—"

"It wasn't just about the pie. It was about the fundraiser and how hard people worked, and you sort of ruined that for them. So, you and Sammy baked a bunch of cookies to raise money for your own donation. Then, you each wrote a letter apologizing for what you'd done. Sometimes you can show how much you care by putting in some effort instead of just words."

He was right. I couldn't expect a simple apology to be enough, but Alex wouldn't even let me do that without an all-out fight. "I get what you're saying, but I just don't know what to do."

"Or maybe you do know what to do, but you are just afraid to do it, little girl."

My mouth flew open, and he grinned. "I have faith in you, honey. You have a good heart." Wrapping an arm around my shoulders, he said, "I'm sure you'll figure this all out."

Guilt tainted the warm and comforting feeling my dad's hugs always brought. He hadn't even asked me who it was or what had happened. Just supported me like he always did. Hesitantly, I said, "Dad...I need to tell you something."

He pulled back, looked me in the eyes. "What is it, sweetheart?"

"Well..." I took a deep breath, praying my dad would continue to be supportive even after he heard my confession. "The thing about this guy... He's really important to me. In fact, he's—"

"Hey, you two! Hogging the driveway just so you can chit chat?"

Dad and I turned to find Mom walking up from behind the car.

"We're changing the oil," Dad said.

"You just changed the oil last week." She kissed my dad on the cheek, then gave me a hug.

"Dad!" I said, my eyes wide.

He didn't hide his wry smile. "We're bonding, Sue," he said to her but was looking at me.

"Actually, I was about to tell Dad something, but now that you're here—"

"It's going to have to wait," she said, taking me by the wrist. "I need to speak to Ava inside. Your dad will finish, right, dear?"

"Oh, sure, Dad will clean up the mess."

With Mom's grip tightening on my arm, I resisted and gave my dad an apologetic look.

"Go, it's fine," he said. "I'll be in soon."

Without releasing me, Mom went through the front

door and all the way to the kitchen. Then she let go and set her bag down on the counter. "Why don't you wait to tell your dad until this whole thing plays out."

My jaw dropped. "You know? Did...Alex tell you?"

She moved to the fridge and opened the door. "He came to see me today, but I already knew, honey. I have for a while now." After a beat of silence, she shut the door. "I think we'll order pizza tonight. You staying?"

"Mom!" I couldn't think of anything else to say, though I had so many questions. Instinctively, I moved closer to her, and she took me into her arms.

"I'm sorry, baby. I know this is hard for you. For both of you. But I just know in my heart you'll get through it."

With my face against her shoulder, I said, "Aren't you mad at me?"

She chuckled. "Of course not. Do I approve of keeping secrets? No." Then she was quiet, but I stayed in her arms for a few seconds longer before pulling back.

"And?" I asked, sure she must have more to say.

"There's no point hashing it out. We can't help who we love, and to be honest, I saw this coming a mile away. Even when you were with Mark."

I coughed out a laugh, my eyes watering over. "But you know what I did."

Rubbing my back, she said, "Yes, and knowing you, you're punishing yourself enough."

I should have thanked her, but I didn't. I knew what she would say, but I asked what I really wanted to know. "So...what did Alex say to you?"

She pulled her lips beneath her teeth, then said, "I'm not getting in the middle of this, honey. All I can say is give him some time."

Time I could do, but time could also mean... "But what if I give him time, and he gets over me?"

She grinned instantly. "I don't think there's much chance of that."

Chapter Thirty-Six

Alex

The sun had set at least an hour ago, but this was the earliest I'd left the office in months. As I made my way to my car, I saw a dark figure standing nearby, and I tensed. I didn't need any trouble tonight. *It's probably just a vagrant looking for money.* But as I drew closer, I recognized the man waiting for me, the dim lighting from the lot illuminating his face.

"Sammy, what are you doing out here?"

"I was about to come up..." He shoved his hand into the pocket of his jeans. "You got a minute?"

"Yeah," I said hesitantly. I'd made a decision to fix this disaster my life had become, and I was determined to see it through, but I also couldn't ignore the look on Sammy's face. Despite how pissed he was at me, the things he'd said to me, he was my brother.

He let out a loud sigh and looked beyond me toward my office building. "I'm surprised you're leaving this early."

He was stalling, and I didn't have time for that. "What's on your mind, man?"

He shook his head. "I said some shitty things to you..."

I didn't respond, just waited to see what else he had to say.

Returning his focus to me, he said. "But, fuck, man. How could you keep something like that from me?"

I shot him a look that answered him clearly.

"I don't care. You could have trusted me...from the beginning." He rubbed a hand over his jaw. "At least then I could wrap my brain around you two, instead of being blindsided."

Nodding, I said, "I know. And I'm sorry. I fucked up... in more ways than one, but..." I glanced away from the pain in his face. "I know how everyone sees me, and I knew none of you would think I was good enough for Ava, so I—"

"What the hell are you talking about?"

His angered tone had me snapping my gaze back to him. "What do you mean?"

"Alex, bro, you're an idiot, you know that?"

"Come on, man. You think the family would have been behind me and Ava?"

He shook his head. "Hell, I don't know—but not because you're not good enough. Geez, you're clueless. Don't you even see how much you are a part of this family? How important you are?"

"Yeah, the charity case you guys took in because I was your best friend." I pulled my key fob from my pocket, wanting to wrap this up. Admittedly, I needed to face my past, but it had been a long day, and Sammy had caught me off guard.

His brows rose. "Okay, yeah, maybe at first. But you earned your spot...even if you didn't have to. You were there for every single one of us at one time or another. I mean, damn, I've even been jealous a few times when Mom and Dad doted on you like you were the prize son of the family."

I drew my head back, blown away by his revelation. "Bullshit."

Stepping closer, he said, "No...it's the truth, man. But even if there were times like that, there were way more times I was grateful I had a brother like you, one I was proud of, someone who had my back...who helped me watch out for my sister." He paused and I braced for it. "So, yeah, it was shocking to hear, and I was hurt you didn't tell me, but...I guess...I get why you didn't want anyone to know."

"Thank you for saying that." I let out a relieved sigh but still felt sadness in my chest. "I can't lose you, any of you. I thought waiting to tell you was the right thing, but I was stupid, I guess."

He quirked a half grin. "Yeah, well it wasn't the first time."

"True. And it won't be the last."

"For what it's worth, I hope you and Ava work this out." He chuckled. "You and I both know she hasn't exactly picked the right men."

I cocked my head. "I don't know. I just think no one was good enough for us."

"Until now. It still burns, I'll be honest, but I couldn't pick a better man for her." Sammy put a hand on my shoulder. "And listen, Alex, Ava's heart was in the right place. Over the years she and I...we've struggled with this thing with your mom. We didn't want to push, and damn, maybe we should have because you can be a stubborn ass."

"Thanks."

"I'm serious. How long are you going to let this eat away at you?"

"I...I don't know." I let out a huff. "Old habits of denial. Listen, I get it and I know things have to change.

I'm not trying to shut you out, but just trust me when I say I'm working up to something."

"With your mom?" he said with eyes wide. "Or with Ava?"

I took a beat before answering. "Both. As long as I have my bro by my side?"

He held his arms out wide. "No matter what happens, brother."

We hugged it out, and I got into my car. "I've got some things to take care of, but I'll be in touch."

He nodded. "Good because Cass told me not to come home until we were good."

"We're good. And thanks, brother."

I watched Sammy walk to his car and get in before I headed home, feeling a sense of security that my family was intact. And certain of what I needed to do next. At my place, I ate, did some work, and got things ready for the next day.

Rising early, I only grabbed a cup of coffee before heading out the door. The drive would give me time to think things through, gain my courage, find the words I needed to say.

When I arrived at my destination, I was jittery and uncertain. Coffee and no food hadn't helped, so I grabbed a quick sandwich at a small café. While I sat, I scrolled through some of the texts I'd ignored from Ava. It was a jackass move to shut her out like that, but I couldn't deal with the emotions that came with reading her words. But now, I read every one. The apologies. The explanations. The hard truths about me. She never got mean or petty; that wasn't Ava. As hard as it was to read how she felt, it was also somewhat healing. Most of all it made me miss her, my heart clenching as I pictured her waking up to an empty bed. She'd given me everything that night, and I'd selflessly taken what I needed without concern for her. If that didn't prove her love for me, I didn't know what would.

What I did know was that Ava was the only woman for me, and it was time to make this right. Time to cleanse the poison keeping us apart, time to give myself to her completely.

Leaving the café, determination in my gut, I strode down the street with purpose. I arrived at my destination a few blocks later and knocked on the door.

When it opened moments later, she stood in the doorway, shock on her face.

I swallowed, mustered my courage, and said, "Hello, Mom."

Chapter Thirty-Seven

Alex

My pulse quickened at the sight of my mother standing in front of me. Yes, I had seen her for a brief moment in Vegas when Ava and I were there, but I was so angry and caught off guard then. I hadn't had a chance to take in her appearance. She looked older, of course, wrinkles around her eyes and mouth, but her hair was dyed blond, so I didn't know if she would be showing gray yet.

We stared at each other for a few beats, and then my mother stuttered out, "Alex... What are you... I— Would you like to come in?" She opened the door wider and waited.

I stepped inside, saying as I passed her, "I'm sorry I didn't call first."

It seemed the right response when showing up unannounced, but it felt awkward to be so formal with the woman who gave birth to me.

Her house was small and an older model, probably twenty-five to thirty years old. But I could see it was nicely decorated as I guardedly swept my eyes around the room. My heart stuttered against my ribs when I saw a mantel full of pictures of me, some she could have only gotten from Ava or off the internet, but they were displayed like any other family's portraits.

Behind me, she said, "Why don't we sit out back?"

I glanced over my shoulder and watched as she moved into the kitchen area. I stayed in place, suddenly worried this might have been a mistake.

Almost as if she sensed it, she stopped and turned to me, her expression mirroring my feelings. Then, she lifted her mouth into a smile and said, "Can I get you something to drink? I have some fresh tea in the fridge."

I drew in a breath of courage and replied, "That sounds good."

From a distance I watched her go to the fridge and open the door, a quick flash of memory coming to mind of her getting my snack after school.

As she pulled out glasses and then poured the tea, I took a few steps closer.

When she was done, she led me to the back patio, and we each took a seat at a white plastic table with matching chairs that had what appeared to be homemade cushions.

"How are you doing?" she said timidly.

The thought of her skimming the family's socials and the fact that Ava was feeding her information popped into my head. "Pretty good, but then you already knew that, right?" When her face fell, I picked up my tea and said, "I'm sorry."

"Please, don't apologize. Yes, I've seen pictures of you online, but seeing information and images on social media doesn't really give a clear picture of someone's life."

"But you had more than that..."

She knew I was talking about Ava. "The last couple years, yes. But honestly, our contact was minimal." She paused, then added, "I was so glad to hear that you and Ava are seeing each other, though." She grinned as if trying to tempt me into another direction. "She's such a kind and lovely young woman."

"We're not together."

Her eyes narrowed as confusion set in. "Oh... I'm sorry."

I shouldn't have blurted that out, and as I sat there and watched the woman who was basically a stranger to me, I realized I did it out of spite. "I don't really want to talk about it. It wasn't why I came."

Realization seemed to dawn on her, and her eyes fell to her lap. "I am so sorry. It seems as though whether I am in your life or not, I'm ruining things for you. For what it's worth, I practically begged her not to tell you."

We were both quiet for a few minutes, and I was beginning to regret doing this. But how could I just get up and walk away?

"Why did you come?" she finally said.

I sighed. "I don't really know. I guess I got tired of running, so to speak."

Nodding, she said, "I want you to know that I never wanted to leave you. I just knew it was better if I wasn't in your life."

"So, you chose to leave?"

"Of course not." Pain took over her expression. "I would've done anything to make it up to you"—my breathing labored as I thought about the accident and could see she was doing the same—"to be a better mother, the kind of mother you deserved, but your father...he gave me no choice. Either way I wouldn't be with you. It was either jail or leave on my own."

As the years went by, I thought less and less of my mother, but as I sat there listening to her, I was surprised that instead of anger, I felt sorry for her. After all, I lived most of my life with loving people around me, including a woman who was like a mother to me. Before I could say anything, she spoke again.

"Don't get me wrong, my actions were my own, but your father isn't innocent in all this, and that's all I'm going to say on that matter."

I cocked my head, my jaw clenching at the mention of my father. "No. I don't know why I came here, but now that I am here, I would like some answers. If I'm ever going to move on from this, I need to know everything."

She took her gaze from me, stared out to her small yard. "I... I don't feel right talking about a man when he's no longer with us to defend himself."

"If you speak the truth, then there's nothing to defend. Please, I need to know. I need to know everything."

She turned back to me then, her gaze connecting with mine. The pain I saw there was real and deeply rooted. "I was an addict when I met your father. I was an addict when we got married. And I was still an addict when we had you." She shook her head. "But I swear to God, I was clean when I was pregnant with you, not even a drink. You were the only thing that mattered to me." She drew in a deep breath. "Then I had postpartum depression, and... your father didn't seem to want to acknowledge that. He deemed me going through withdrawal, which could have been partially true, but what did that matter?" She was on the verge of tears. "You know how controlling he was. The expectations he had for me as a mother, as a wife. The pressure got to me, and I relapsed."

Without realizing it, I blurted, "I'm sorry." Maybe part of me felt my existence caused her ultimate downfall.

Reaching out, she touched my hand on the table. "You were such a good little boy, Alex. I tried. I really did. And I would have weeks and months of sobriety and then... something would happen with your father, and I'd slip."

"Something?" I feared the worst, like there was something she wasn't saying. "Please, I have to know."

"Look, I know I wasn't the best wife. I was a burden to your dad."

"What did he do?" My anger bubbled to the surface, and in front of me I saw the woman who begged me to run from that accident, who wanted to save me. "Did he hurt you?"

She shook her head. "No, nothing like that. He... He wasn't happy with me so...he found his happiness elsewhere, with other women."

My heart broke for her, this woman who had made mistakes but also fell victim to my father. "I had no idea. I'm sorry."

"It's not your fault." She sighed and sipped her drink, as if she were trying to wash away the grief. "The day of the accident, he told me he was going to take you from me, and I guess I just snapped. I was stupid and reckless, and I'll regret my actions for the rest of my life."

I shook my head. "I don't know what to say except, thank you for telling me."

We were quiet for a short time when she said, "I understand if this was all you came for, Alex, but I want you to know not a day has gone by that I haven't thought of you...that I haven't prayed to God you were all right, happy. I love you, Son, whether you want to hear that or not."

I was speechless, my heart strained, my pulse racing in my veins, and I longed to reach out to my mom and be that little boy from so long ago, before it all turned horrible. My silence must have triggered her because she rose abruptly.

"I guess you want to go now."

When she started for the door, I stood. "Mom, wait."

Her back to me, she froze. When she turned slowly to face me, her eyes were filled with tears. "Yes?"

"I don't want to go. I'd like to spend some more time with you, if that's all right."

She smiled and walked back over.

We stood face to face, and after a few beats, we both pulled each other in. My mother held me like she never wanted to let me go, and as emotion clogged my throat, I held her just as tightly.

Chapter Thirty-Eight

Ava

With the bathtub filling beside me, I peered at my haggard face in the mirror. I didn't know if the puffy red eyes were from lack of sleep, or all the stress and sadness since the blowup between Alex and me. I had stopped trying to call him, stopped leaving messages, especially after I went to his office, and they said he was out of town—and he hadn't even told me. Mom had said to give him space, and I wished I'd taken her advice sooner. Maybe then I wouldn't feel so hopeless. And, admittedly, a little pissed off, even if I had no right to be.

Sighing, I moved back to the tub. As I turned the water off, I heard Gunnar coming down the hall. "I'll get it," he called, although I hadn't heard the door since the water was running. But I had also left my phone out there and wondered if he was planning to answer it. *I hope not.*

So, I leaned in and listened, then a beat later, I heard him say, "Keep that water warm for me, baby, and I'll join you in a minute."

I cracked the door open, my eyes narrowed in confusion. Then I heard what sounded like the front door slamming against the inside wall. I tightened the tie on my robe and raced out to the living room, where I found Alex pressing Gunnar up against the open door, holding him by the collar of his shirt.

"Hey!" I said, glaring at Alex.

He turned his head to me, his eyes quickly scanning my half-naked body and then narrowing. "Fuck this!" he said, then pushed off of Gunnar and turned to the doorway.

"Wait a minute!" I didn't know what was going on, but I wasn't about to let him walk out like that.

He spun and glared at me.

I turned an expectant gaze to a breathless Gunnar, who was straightening his shirt.

Likely out of pure self-preservation, Gunnar quickly piped up with, "Alex, man I was just screwing with you." He shook his head, then headed toward the hallway. "I'm sure you two have lots to talk about."

My heart still racing, I watched Gunnar's retreating back until he disappeared behind his door.

When I turned back to Alex, the first thing that hit me was his expression—guilt or shame that lasted only a few seconds before he dropped his chin to his chest and shook his head. "I should have known..."

"Yeah, you should have. Or do you have such little faith in me that you think I would do that to you?" I folded my arms, annoyed he played the jealousy card after ignoring me for days.

Closing the door, he said, "No, I don't. That was just a stupid knee-jerk reaction."

"Really?"

He nodded and stepped toward me. It took everything in me not to leap into his arms. I couldn't put myself out there...not yet at least. Instead, I said, "What are you doing here?"

Another step had us almost toe to toe, and I caught his gaze dip to the V in my robe before snapping up to meet mine. "God, I missed you." It came out in barely a whisper, so I wasn't sure he'd even said the words.

I held my breath, waiting for more.

Bending forward, he brought his face closer to mine, but I didn't move. We stood that way, staring at each other, the only sound our breathing growing more labored.

When his hand reached up and brushed down my cheek, I pulled back.

Then I took a step toward the hallway. "If this is some sort of a booty call, you can forget it."

His hand caught my wrist before I'd even finished the sentence. "It's not," he said through a chuckle. Then he head-gestured to the couch. "Please?"

I nodded and let him lead me around the couch—ignoring how needy I felt with my hand in his—and then we both sat, turning our bodies toward each other.

He ran a hand through his hair and sighed. "I'm sorry..."

"No, I'm sorry," I blurted, though I wasn't totally sure what he was apologizing for. "I betrayed your trust."

He nodded. "But you did it out of love, and the way I acted...that was me being an ass."

I raised my brows and added a little head cock to show I agreed but added, "You were hurt."

"I was...and you forced me to think about something I've been hiding from...for too long."

"But that's your choice, Alex." I scooted closer and placed a hand on his knee. "I didn't plan what happened, and I know I should have told you, but no matter when you found out, you would have been upset..."

"I know. Everything just felt...out of control. But now

—well—I think you did me a favor." A half grin rose on his face.

"What do you mean?"

"I went to see my mom." As if he knew I'd be pleased, his grin grew.

"Really?" When he nodded, I threw my arms around his neck. "Oh, Alex, I'm so proud of you." His arms pulling me to him felt like the sign I needed that everything was going to be all right.

Though I didn't want to let him go, I was anxious to hear more, so I pulled back. "Did you...want to tell me about it?"

He chuckled. "We had a long talk. She told me things I didn't remember, things I never knew about." He shook his head. "My dad played a bigger part in my disastrous family than I ever realized." His expression turned dark then. "My mother made some terrible choices, and she let me down...but she didn't deserve a lifetime of me shutting her out."

Shaking my head, I took his hand. "Hey, don't blame yourself for that. Most of those years, you had no choice. Now you have the rest of your life to make up for lost time." I paused, peering into his eyes. "That is what you want?" I asked hesitantly.

He shrugged a shoulder. "I want her in my life...but I want to take it slow. Right now, I have other priorities."

"You do?" I grinned.

"Yeah, I should probably apologize to Gunnar," he said matter-of-factly.

My mouth fell open. "Oh…"

When he released a bark of laughter, I sighed in relief, then smacked him in the chest. At the same time he hooked me by the waist and pulled me against him, his mouth capturing mine. It felt like home and hope and heat all wrapped up in one deep, delicious kiss.

Alex ended the kiss but kept me a breath away from him. "I should really apologize to Gunnar, too, though."

I shook my head, holding back a devious grin. "Let him sweat it out. Teach him a lesson for messing with you."

"That's my girl," he said.

Hearing him call me his girl sent a flush of heat over my skin, but I didn't have time to recover because Alex rose to his feet, then bent to pick me up. I wrapped my arms around his neck, my legs around his waist as he walked me down the hall.

"I love you," he whispered into my ear.

"I love you."

Closing the door behind us, he pressed me against the back of my bedroom door. "Hang on, baby. We've got a lot of time to make up for."

Chapter Thirty-Nine

Alex

Ava slid onto my lap and wrapped her arms around my neck just as Sammy and Sue walked into the dining room, each carrying a tray of food.

"Aw, come on," Sammy groaned. "Can we have some more acclimation before we have to see that?"

"We weren't even doing anything," Ava said, then lifted a brow. "Yet."

They set the trays on the table as Sue said, "I think it's lovely...and it makes me happy." She turned and ran a hand over our heads like we were her sweet, innocent children.

"Wow, guess we know who your favorite child is," Sammy said with an edge in his tone.

"Oh, stop." Sue waved a hand at Sammy. "I'm just so grateful we're all together for the holiday. It's going to be the best Thanksgiving." She moved around the table, closer to Sammy, and nudged his shoulder. "Now go grab the rest of those plates."

"Hey, why don't they have to help?" Sammy glared at us, and I grinned back, loving the pouty expression, even if he was milking it.

"I do believe you were still asleep when Ava and me were chopping up a storm this morning," I said.

Ava stood and gave her best "Yea-ahh!" with a hand on her hip.

I had to admit, this whole scene felt right, comfortable, warming something inside me I'd kept somewhat guarded over the years. And it was a welcome distraction for my nerves. Then the doorbell rang, and we all froze and went wide-eyed.

Sue patted her hair like her prom date had just arrived. "Oh, goodness, that's her."

I stood, and Ava shot me a sweet grin as she slipped her hand in mine. "You all right?"

I nodded but then my head flooded with thoughts as I looked at each of their faces, trying to get my feet to move. There was no turning back after today. I reminded myself I wasn't losing a family, just making room for one more.

I must have been in my head too long because Sue

said, "I've got it" and then patted my shoulder as she walked by me.

"Wait!" My abrupt tone stopped her in her tracks, and she turned back to me.

"What is it, dear?"

I slipped away from Ava's and went to Sue's side. "I just want to say... Well, you've been..." I shook my head. "No matter what..."

A giant smile formed on her face. "I know, honey. I love you too... Even if you are doing the nasty between the sheets with my baby girl."

My eyes widened, and everyone else gasped.

Sue shrugged. "What? I was trying to lighten the mood."

The doorbell rang again, and Denny appeared then from the hallway. "No one's getting that?"

"I'm going," Sue said, walking toward the door.

I knew I was being ridiculous. It wasn't like I was going to hide from her all afternoon. I turned my gaze on Denny, and he gave me a single nod, saying, "You've got this, Son."

I returned the nod, then took off in Sue's wake. She already had the door open when I rounded the corner, and I watched as the two women exchanged a hug, my mother's eyes connecting with mine over Sue's shoulder.

I grinned and moved up to them. "Hi..." Leaning in, I

gave her an awkward hug. I didn't know why I couldn't bring myself to say "Mom." I'd said it before, but in front of Sue it would take a minute.

"Thank you both for having me," my mother said quietly when I pulled back.

"Of course, Maggie. You're always welcome here," Sue said.

It was then I noticed she was holding a bag at her side. "I brought a few things," she said, lifting it.

"Wonderful. Why don't we take it to the kitchen?"

Sue led the way, followed by my mother and then me. In the doorway of the kitchen, Sue turned and said, "Alex, can you and Sammy grab the extra chairs from the garage? Denny forgot." She gave me a half grin, and I breathed a sigh of relief, offering my own smile of gratitude for the break.

"Sure..."

When I hesitated, she added, "We'll be just fine."

For some reason, I looked to my mother then, feeling an unexpected sense of obligation to make sure she was comfortable.

She grinned and nodded her approval, then said to Sue, "I'd love to help with whatever you need."

Sammy and I quickly gathered the chairs and placed them at the table. We could hear all four women in the kitchen, talking and laughing as if they'd all been doing it for years.

"You know this means we're outnumbered, bro," Sammy said with a head gesture toward the kitchen.

I barked out a chuckle. "I hadn't thought of that."

"I'm married. I always think of that." His smile faded as he stepped closer. "Hey...I know I've been giving you a lot of shit lately."

I cocked my head to the side. "Payback's a bitch, right?"

"Yeah, you deserve it, but"—he gripped my shoulder, hard—"I'm ready to let it all go, as long as..."

"What?"

"I know the days of us making life hard for Ava's boyfriends is over, but I'll come out of retirement if I have to."

I let out a hearty laugh and deliberately removed his hand. "That won't be necessary, man. You know that, right? Shit, I hope you do." I released an unsteady breath, but I was ready to put it out there for him. "This is it for me, Sammy. *She's* it for me." I held his gaze.

"I know." He nodded. "I just wanted to hear you say it."

For a second, I felt for all the poor schmucks we'd tortured in the past, but then I grinned and said, "I'm starving."

We both laughed and headed into the kitchen to join the women. Cass and Dax had come in from the backyard and the whole scene—everyone snacking and chatting, smiles all around, felt so perfect.

Denny eventually came out to join us, just as we all finally gathered around the table. I sat between Ava and my mother, with Sue across from me, not an ounce of uncertainty in her sweet smile. Denny said a quick prayer, and once we all had our plates filled, we went around the table as we ate, sharing all the blessings we were thankful for. When it came to my turn, I had no shortage of things to say. In that moment, I felt the most blessed I'd ever been in my whole life.

Chapter Forty

Ava

Alex hung back by the entry as Gunnar and I chatted with a few of the dancers backstage. We were both as giddy as two kids meeting Mickey at Disneyland, even though we'd both been in their position as dancers in this venue ourselves. I was a little worried that coming to Vegas and seeing all my friends still performing in shows was going to feel like a blow, but it didn't. I was just grateful to see their beautiful faces again, and I didn't have an ounce of regret for the current state of my life.

Kieran rubbed a hand over Gunnar's bicep. "Boy, you still got it. Not even letting yourself go."

"Please, I'll never neglect this body," Gunnar said matter-of-factly.

As our friends laughed, I glanced over at Alex, who rolled his eyes. I was actually surprised he'd been the one to invite Gunnar on this trip with us. Given it was an early birthday present for me, I appreciated it.

When we said our goodbyes, I heard Claire say to Gunnar, "See you in a bit."

I assumed she was talking about the after-party Sydney was having, but Claire had a new baby, so it seemed odd she'd go. I was sure Alex would not want to attend, but by the time I thought about making an excuse, Gunnar was suddenly ushering me out of there.

We made our way to our seats, which were perfectly selected for the best view and experience. Not the front row but just a few rows back. Gunnar was on the aisle, then Alex next to him and then me. I noticed the two of them were chatting while I checked some things on my phone. Grinning, I mused how lucky I was to have two such wonderful men in my life. The last six months—since Alex and I found our way back to each other—had been pure bliss. It was almost like a brand-new courtship. We went on dates, got to know new things about each other, and had some of the most incredible nights together.

I felt Alex's lips next to my cheek. "Do you know how

amazing you are?" He placed a soft kiss behind my ear, sending chills over my skin.

I flinched and giggled like a school girl. "Alex!" I turned my head so our gazes connected. Then quieter, I said, "I love you."

He leaned in until his lips were just brushing mine. "I love you more..."

"Thank you for the trip."

He smiled. "I just love seeing you so happy... We can come here anytime you want, you know."

I nodded. "I know. Honestly, as great as it is to see everyone, it also solidifies everything I've been feeling lately."

His smile faltered, and his brows knitted. "Oh? What's that?"

I touched his cheek. "That I'm the happiest I've ever been...and it's all because of you."

He took my hand in his, then, and interlaced our fingers. "I feel the same way." When he leaned in for another kiss, Gunnar coughed loudly, and we both turned that way.

"Not that I'm feeling like a third wheel or anything, but the show's going to start any minute."

"Sorry, Gunnar," I said, leaning forward to see him better. "Maybe if we go to Sydney's after party, you'll meet someone." Alex could tough it out for a bit, I figured.

"Besides the fact that I don't do long-distance relationships, I doubt we'll make it to the party."

I narrowed my gaze on him. "What? Why?" When I darted my eyes to Alex, he looked annoyed.

Then Gunnar rushed to say, "I, uh, just meant we might get distracted, you know..." The lights faded and Gunnar pointed toward the stage. "Shh, it's starting."

Everything fell away when the music started, and I immersed myself in the experience. Of course, I could still envision myself up on that stage, but I instead chose to focus on my friends and how well they were doing, and how most of them, like myself, were already working toward a new life away from entertainment.

Toward the end of the show, Alex leaned in and whispered, "Be right back?"

Figuring he had to go to the restroom, I said, "It's almost over."

His mouth pulled into a tight line, and he grimaced. "Sorry, can't wait."

I tilted my head to see Gunnar shrug and then move so Alex could get out. But then they both walked off. I hoped Gunnar wouldn't miss the end, a chance to see the light shining on our friends' faces when they took that final bow.

A few minutes later, the music faded, and the boys still hadn't returned. Our friend Kieran took center stage as the other dancers ran off, and I furrowed my brow. This wasn't typical for this show.

"Ladies and gentlemen, we have a special treat for you tonight if you'd like to stick around for just another few minutes."

"Oh, God," I whispered under my breath as the audience clapped and cheered. They can't possibly think I am in any position to get up there and dance. Could they? I shook the thought away. That would be ridiculous.

Kieran turned her head to the side and announced, "We have a very special guest tonight, and he has something important to share with all of you...especially one very special woman."

He? I followed her line of sight, and my heart stopped. Alex was walking onto the stage. "What the—"

Stopping front and center, Alex took the mic from Kieran, and then his gaze homed right in on me. "Baby... I've loved you most of my life, and I can't believe how damn lucky I am to finally be with you."

"Whoo!" someone shouted from the audience. "Yeah, man!"

Alex let his sexy grin out and continued. "You mean everything to me, Ava. Everything." I covered my mouth with one of my hands, then felt someone touching me. My friend Claire took me by the wrist and led me toward the stage as Alex continued. "I can't imagine my life without you and just want to make you smile. Which is why you're the only person in the world who can bring this out of me..."

As Claire led me up the stairs and seated me in a chair, Alex handed the mic back to Kieran. Then music began to play as all the dancers flitted around the stage getting in formation behind Alex. I laughed as my eyes glazed over with tears when I realized the song was "The Time of My Life" probably since we'd recently watched *Dirty Dancing*, and I'd told him how much I love the song and the movie.

Holy crap, this is not happening. Except it was. Alex might not have been a professional dancer, but my man had moves and was so damn sexy he had the whole audience cheering for him. I laughed when I caught sight of Gunnar behind him with the other dancers.

It wasn't long before Alex came to me, swept me from the chair and held me in his arms. We swayed to the music, and he whispered in my ear. "I hope this is okay..."

I pulled back and locked gazes with him. "Okay?" I laughed. "It's a dream come true."

We swayed and grinned and kissed, and just before the song started to fade, he reached into his pocket and then lowered to one knee. "Ava, please, make all my dreams come true and marry me. I promise I'll spend every day of my life making yours come true too."

I nodded and barely choked out a "yes" before he slid the ring over my finger. Then I pulled him up, and his lips went right to mine. The kiss we shared held so much emotion, so many promises, and the best feeling of all...I knew Alex would come through on every single one.

About the Author

Bestselling author Lia Fairchild writes romance and women's fiction. Fans of her books praise her endearing, real characters who come to life in stories that will touch your heart.

Fairchild is addicted to the warmth of Southern California and holds a bachelor's degree in journalism and a multiple-subject teaching credential. She is a wife and mother of two.